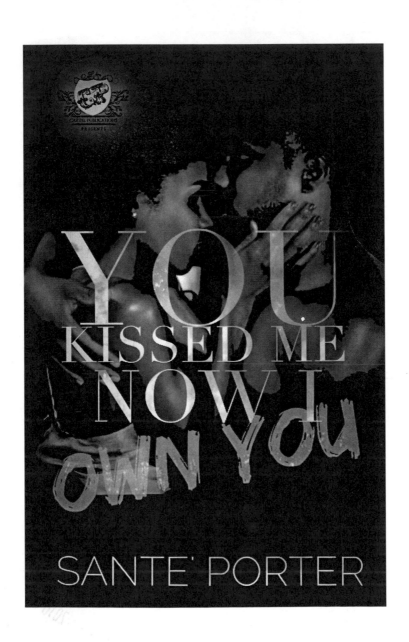

YOU KISSED ME NOW I OWN YOU

SANTE' PORTER

By Sante' Porter

ARE YOU ON OUR EMAIL LIST?

SIGN UP ON OUR WEBSITE

www.thecartelpublications.com

OR TEXT THE WORD:

CARTELBOOKS TO 22828

FOR PRIZES, CONTESTS, ETC.

4   By Sante' Porter

LIPSTICK DOM
A SCHOOL OF DOLLS
KALI: RAUNCHY RELIVED THE MILLER FAMILY
SKEEZERS
YOU KISSED ME NOW I OWN YOU
THE END. HOW TO WRITE A BESTSELLING NOVEL IN 30 DAYS

WWW.THECARTELPUBLICATIONS.COM

YOU KISSED ME, NOW I OWN YOU

By

Santé Porter

Library of Congress Control Number: 2015960729

ISBN 10: 0996209980

ISBN 13: 9780996209984

Cover Design: Bookslutgirl.com

www.thecartelpublications.com
First Edition
Printed in the United States of America

What's Up Fam,

Merry Christmas and happy holidays to you and your family! I hope you enjoy this little surprise treat we dropped on you. ;)

"You Kissed Me, Now I Own You" is FULL of drama! I know you gonna get a kick out of it just as much as I did so enjoy!

With that being said and keeping in line with tradition, we want to give respect to a vet or a trailblazer paving the way. In this novel, we would like to recognize:

T.D. Jakes

Bishop Thomas Dexter Jakes, Sr. is a Pastor, Filmmaker and Author. He has penned several novels, too many to list. However, "Destiny: Step Into Your Purpose" is the latest in his arsenal of books to aid in the betterment of your life. On a personal note, in recent months, Bishop Jakes' messages have personally touched me and have helped to restore my faith. I hope that whether you are going through a personal storm of your own or not, you can find comfort and healing in his words too.

By Sante' Porter

Aight, get to it. I'll catch you in the next novel.

Be Easy!

Charisse "C. Wash" Washington

Vice President

The Cartel Publications

www.thecartelpublications.com

www.facebook.com/publishercwash

Instagram: publishercwash

www.twitter.com/cartelbooks

www.facebook.com/cartelpublications

Follow us on Instagram: Cartelpublications

#CartelPublications

#UrbanFiction

#TDJakes

#PrayForCeCe

CHAPTER ONE

PAIGE

"I should've never trusted that bitch," Paige said to herself as she walked toward her boss's door. Her only friend in the world, Asia, warned her against trusting new chicks at the club but she wanted to give Darla the benefit of the doubt. And look where it led her...possibly unemployed.

The thing was there was no time for thinking of what she'd done wrong. She had to remember the conversations she overheard in the locker room about how *he* liked it *kissed* and *licked*. After all there wasn't a girl on staff who hadn't paid their dues sexually, but her.

Until now.

If she played her hand right maybe she wouldn't have to go so far. After all she was his favorite.

Entering his office without knocking, Paige was attempting to see if there was something she could say to

By Sante' Porter

convince her boss to let her stay. It wasn't like she hit the whole register for the night's profit. It was just a few bucks to cover rent. But when Darla walked in on her tucking fifties in her jean pocket she thought it was best to tell her the truth instead of lie. Surely Darla would understand since she was a mother with five kids at home herself. Instead she learned that Darla would use the information of Paige's theft against her, just to gain favor with their boss.

Paige Lewis worked as a stripper and part time cashier on her off days for the Daniel Johnson's strip club for two years. She was told by a few of the dancers coming in and out, that he'd changed strippers like he did shoes. But after lasting for the first year, earning more seniority than any other dancer, they recanted their stories saying that maybe she was special.

Besides, Paige did a hell of a job. Danny didn't want for anything in between her sets. His breakfast, lunch and even dinner was all taken care of by Paige. Although she didn't pay for anything out of pocket, Danny gave her access to his funds and as a result, she took excellent care of him. It was her financial expertise and experience that prevented him from pushing himself on her so aggressively like he did some of his other exotic dancers. Her goal was simple. Be irreplaceable, and he found her invaluable.

But late last night, armed with the news of her theft, he approached her ferociously when the club was empty. He walked up behind her and told her how beautiful she was and how much he desired her. But when she rejected him, he became angry. Part of running the club was living his fantasy of having sex with a bevy of women but Paige was always off limits, until she stole from him.

"You're fired, Paige. You're free to get your things tomorrow but after that I never want to see you in this club again."

Tears rolling down her face she asked, "Sir, what did I do? You know I need this job! I have twin—"

"You stole from me." He interrupted. "Be glad the respect I have for you prevents me from calling the cops."

It was final.

She was terminated.

By Sante' Porter

She tried to explain that running the register, like he preferred because she was the only one he trusted with the money, didn't net as much cash as dancing. But he was unreasonable and didn't care.

He threw her away without thinking about her children and the responsibility she had to keep them safe and fed.

When she entered his office he was on the phone. She felt what she was preparing to do was cause enough to interrupt him.

"How can I help you, Paige?" He said in an authoritative voice knowing full well she wanted to plead her case. "Can't you see I'm busy?"

"Sir...may I talk to you?" Paige asked as if she was a six-year-old little girl asking for candy. "I'd like to kick it with you for a moment."

"I'll call you back," He said to his caller before hanging up. "Make it quick. I have a lot of work to do around here."

She reluctantly walked deeper inside his office and gave him a half-hearted smile. She was trying her best to give off the illusion that she wanted to do what her body didn't.

Closing the door and locking it behind herself, she walked even closer.

"How can I help you, Ms. Lewis?"

Her body trembled. *"Well...*I've been thinking." She tried to prevent her tears from flowing due to feeling disgusted at what was to come.

"Thinking what?" He paused. "I said make it quick, girl! I don't have all day!" He slammed a fist onto the top of the desk.

"I've been thinking about you." She unbuttoned her peach blouse with the gold buttons. "And me."

He grinned. "And what have you been thinking about you and me, Ms. Lewis?" He was making her job excruciating.

"I've been thinking that I want you. In fact, sir, I've always wanted you."

He laughed. "Oh really? Because I couldn't tell."

"It's all true, sir and I was wrong for making you wait for me, for so long. You are a hardworking man who

By Sante' Porter

deserves to have anything you desire. And I'm ready to submit. If you'll have me."

"Is that right?"

"Yes it is."

Turning his self around in the chair, he opened his legs back and forth anticipating finally having his way. Besides, Paige was beautiful. Her size 40D breasts and size 10-inch waist made her very appealing. Her apple butter skin was flawless and always appeared to be rosy. She was humble about her sexy physique despite the men around her never letting her forget that her existence alone spelled, 'SEX'.

"Well...what are you waiting for? Get on your knees." He said in a serious tone.

She stopped unbuttoning her blouse and did as she was told. It was obvious that he wanted to get down to business. Paige was insulted by how he was treating her but not surprised. He made it clear from day one what his intentions were. But she always thought by proving how valuable she was, he'd never replace her and that he'd eventually give up trying to pursue her. But now she knew she was wrong.

If only she hadn't hit that register this would not have happened.

"Give me a kiss."

That was the one thing it was hard to do. To Paige kisses were personal and meant for someone she was feeling and this was not that type of party. Instead she dropped to her knees and placed one hand on the top of his thighs. She figured he'd forget about the kiss in a moment and she was right too.

He spared her from having to un-zippen his pants by doing it himself. Exposing his already stiff penis, he stroked it twice before handing it over to her to do the rest.

Why should he help when it was her job?

Paige fought the urge to toss her lunch all over his legs when one thought came to mind. Her kids. Most people would have found it repulsive or inappropriate, and she did too, but she would do anything to see that her sons would not fall victim to the streets…including suck dick.

Taking him into her mouth, she licked him as if she loved him or as if her life depended on it. She was a

By Sante' Porter

professional at giving head having done it for so many years to satisfy whatever man had control over her life at the time. Her last boyfriend made her give him oral sex every night as a condition of staying in the same bed. If she refused or acted like she didn't want to, he would make her sleep in the car or on the floor. If she slept in the car, on cold nights he would throw her a blanket but keep the keys to teach her a lesson.

If only she could have escaped him unattached. It didn't happen. The only time they ever had sex; she got pregnant, resulting in the twins. He had a warped way of thinking because he said that sex was for procreation and not pleasure. Yet he would force her to commit oral satisfaction on him almost every day. But after having her boys, she didn't want them to see how he treated their mother. She started speaking up for herself and demanding respect. But the moment she did, he threw them all out on the streets, never seeing them again. So she kept odd jobs to provide a roof over their heads but she could never fully make ends meet.

Paige worked her boss up so good that within two minutes, he came inside of her mouth. Globs of cum on the seat of her tongue. "Open your lips and let me see that milk," he demanded.

She obeyed.

Seeing his cream nut on her pink tongue almost got him hard again. "Now swallow."

There was no use in arguing. So she obeyed again.

"Good, girl," he winked.

She was humiliated but satisfied that she didn't have to do it so long. When she was done, he reached into his pocket and gave her four hundred dollars in cash.

"That's for your next two weeks. Good luck on your job search." He said pulling himself and his clothing together.

Her eyes widened. "What?" She stuttered. "What are you saying? I thought...I thought..."

"I'm saying good luck on finding a new job. What part don't you understand?"

"But I thought by doing this...you'd let me keep my job here." She said tears rolling down her face. "Please, sir. I need this."

"I never said you could keep your job, Paige." He laughed, zippering his pants and standing up to open the door for her. "Now leave my office."

"Don't do this, Daniel! I'll even work for half the price." She begged.

"It's too late, Paige." He said cruelly and without emotion. "You should have thought about that before making me wait so long. Now get the fuck out of my office! I don't deal with thieves or whores."

Picking up what was left of her pride and the things in her box, she walked out the office, got in her car and cried herself all the way home.

CHAPTER TWO

PAIGE

"I don't know what I'm gonna do, girl. He fucking fired me." They were sitting on two of the only three chairs in the room she rented in Bladensburg, Maryland.

"That's some bullshit. I couldn't stand his ass anyway!" Asia, Paige's best friend said. "He was always looking at me creepy when I came to pick you up and shit." She whipped her long black ponytail over her shoulder.

They'd known each other since high school and she was the closest to family Paige had, besides her estranged aunt Laverne. Having been in foster care after her mother died and then abandoned, Paige never really had family or a home. So Asia was the only person outside of Tone she trusted.

"Well I don't know what I'm gonna do now! For real, Asia. Asshole or not, that was the best job I ever had because the money was steady. How am I gonna pay rent now?" She got up and walked to her bed with Asia following.

"What about Tone's fine ass? He can't help you out?" Asia sat on the edge of Paige's mattress and waited for an answer.

"Girl, you know I don't like asking him for shit. It's bad enough he pays the phone bill and part of my electric." Paige watched her kids, five-year-old twin boys named Marcus and Marco, play on the floor.

"You haven't even kissed him have you?" Asia asked.

Paige frowned. "No, for what?"

"Why are you so serious about this kiss thing? You'd rather suck and fuck a nigga before kissing them."

"I'm not going to tell you because you'll think it's stupid."

"What is it?"

Paige sat next to her and exhaled. "I don't remember a lot about my mother except a story she use to tell me when I was little...Sleeping Beauty."

Asia fell out into laughter and Paige frowned. "You see, that's why I didn't want to tell you shit."

"I'm sorry, girl, go 'head." She tried to stop laughing.

Paige rolled her eyes. "Anyway, my mother said in life you may have to give away a lot as a woman. Even your body. But never kiss a man who you don't intend on being with for the rest of your life. The only reason to ever kiss a man is when you're sure he's your first love, or when you hope he can take you away from your problems. She said it was the most important decision I'd ever have to make and I still believe her."

"So how many people have you kissed?"

"None...not even the twins father."

Asia was shocked because she kissed a rack of niggas in her lifetime. "Wow...kiss or not you gotta do something. You know the bitch you renting from gonna want her money no matter what you going through."

"I know but I can't rely on his married ass either." Paige said sadly. "I want to be taken care of by a man who belongs to me. I mean *really* taken care of. I deserve that shit, Asia. I'd make someone a good woman but I'm done with the games. A nigga gonna have to come at me right or he's gonna have trouble."

"Girl, you preaching to the choir for real." Asia waved her hand in the air. "You know I know. But in the mean time you gonna have to do what you gotta do."

Paige knew Asia was right and it hurt. Her landlord was as understanding and as honest as her ex-boss. She was going to have to think of something quick if she didn't want to be out on the street.

"If you want I can scoop the boys up from school for you and keep them for a few hours while you job search."

"As crazy as you drive? Yeah, right, bitch," Paige joked. "I wish I would let my kids get in your car."

"Fuck you, man!"

While talking to Asia, Paige's phone rang. She hoped it was one of the numbers she'd just called a few hours ago about a job. After leaving the club earlier she went to 7-eleven, grabbed a newspaper and called every secretarial job she saw in the want ads. She decided her stripping days were over and wanted something more professional. She also realized she couldn't waste time finding another job when she had a mountain of bills due.

Time was of the essence.

"Hello." Paige responded hopefully.

"Hey, baby. What you doing tonight? You feel up for company?"

"Oh," she said disappointedly.

"Well I'm happy you excited to hear from me." He laughed. "What's wrong? Somebody fucking with my baby?"

"No." she tried not to sound disappointed again that it was Tone and not an employment opportunity. "I'm just sitting here kicking it with Asia that's all."

"So can I slide by and see you later." He asked in his magnetic tone that used to drive her crazy. "I'm trying to see you tonight for real. I mean...lately you been dogging me, baby girl."

"Not tonight, sweetie. I don't have anybody to watch the kids and I'm not in the mood for any company." She thought about how she lost her job earlier in the day.

"Well look...why don't you let me roll through and bring the kids some pizza. And maybe we can chill together in the car for a minute." He loved playing on the fact that she never passed up a meal for her boys.

She shook her head because once again he got his way. "Okay. I'll see you shortly." She hung up.

Paige kicked it with Asia for a little while before saying goodbye, cleaning her sons up and getting them ready for dinner. She wished her place was large enough to entertain company, but all she could afford right now was a large room. It was tiny but it was clean and big enough for a table, three chairs, a bed, a TV and a dresser. She and her boys slept together in a queen size bed.

As small as it was, Paige was satisfied just as long as her kids didn't have to stay in the streets.

Tone arrived forty-five minutes after calling with pizza in hand. When she opened the door she smiled a little at how happy he was to see her. He was 6'4 roughly and about 210 pounds. Tone's chocolate skin and five o'clock shadow made him very appealing. His body had a purpose. He used to play football in college before injuring himself and now worked as an auto mechanic who dealt a little coke on the side. He wanted to maintain Paige as his only side chick because he knew she would never tell his wife, but Paige couldn't deal with him being married and that made her a challenge.

"Hey you." He moved into the house and toward the room after landing a kiss on her cheek.

"Hey, Tone." Paige whispered, not wanting to wake up the old lady she rented the room from who also lived there. "Thanks for the pizza."

The landlord gave Paige a hard time each month despite the fact that she was never late on rent and her kids were very respectful. Paige knew she was racist and let a lot of stuff she said slide to keep the peace. Primarily because the old bat's home was clean and the neighborhood they lived in was safe. But she made a promise to herself that the moment she left, she'd tell her how she truly felt.

Once in the room the kids jumped up on Tone and gave him a huge hug. He'd won them over a long time ago with gifts and food so they were sold. And since no other man was in their lives he was the closest thing to daddy, something else Paige feared.

"What's up lil knuckle heads? I got ya'll some food and candy!" He said squeezing them both before putting them down.

"Thanks, Uncle Tone!" They sang.

"Ya'll been good right?" He asked already knowing the answer.

"Yes." They said truthfully.

"Well here's some money too." Showing off, he gave them fifty dollars a piece that he knew would go toward any food needed in the house. It was the only way she'd accept any additional money from him for that month.

"Thank you!" They yelled.

"No problem, Twinny-Twins," He joked. After serving the kids he turned to Paige. "You ready to go chill outside?"

"Yeah." She appreciated what he did for the children but didn't want them getting too attached to a man who didn't belong to her. "Let me put the pizza on plates for them real quick."

She was only going in front of the house and since the window was open she could walk up on it and see what they were doing inside. On the way out, they met old lady Clarke in the hallway. "Where you think you going?" She screamed.

Paige rolled her eyes. "Just out front." Paige said real softly.

"Not without them damn kids!" She frowned.

"Mrs. Clarke, I'm just going right out front." She pointed. " I can hear the kids right from the window." She reassured her.

"I don't give a damn what you can hear out there! You can hear 'em even better in your room! What you think this is? A got damn daycare center!" She yelled.

"Ma'am...we're right out front but if it's gonna be a problem, I can pay you right now to let 'em chill . It's not that serious," Tone interjected.

"Fool, I'm not for sale like this little whore of yours!" Her voice grew louder; as she tried to entertain the other tenants who she was certain were listening from inside their rooms. "Now take them ankle biters out there with you or keep your fast ass in here with them, Paige! Your choice!" She waved the walking cane for expression instead of walking.

Mrs. Clarke was very pale and had many wrinkles throughout her white face with the exception of the dark circles around her eyes. She didn't go anywhere without the multi-colored flower housecoat she wore with the tiny silver buttons. They wondered if she ever took it off to wash it or her dirty grey wig. She smelled of hate, loneliness and old dirty clothes and Paige knew if she didn't get a man and a better place to stay, in her old age she'd end up the same way.

In the past Paige tried to win her over by spending time with her but whenever the bitter old woman felt herself letting down her guards, and liking Paige, she would remind Paige that she was a nigger, so Paige stopped trying.

"Like I said we can pay you." Tone reiterated.

"Who do you think you are?" She spat. "You come in here all hours of the night and think you doing something by throwing your dirty money around here? You ain't doing shit! All ya'll ain't nothing but some no good niggers!"

Tone was stunned. "Hold up, what you just say to me?" He took one step closer.

Mrs. Clarke backed up a little knowing full well she'd crossed the line. Sometimes her hatred came out at the wrong time and often got her into more trouble than her age could handle.

"I said…uh…your money ain't no good here!".

"Let me tell you something, I don't know who the fuck you think you talking to, but you better watch your fucking mouth before I make you swallow them beige ass teeth you sucking on." He was threatening and serious and Paige was taken aback.

"Go outside, baby." Paige pleaded, trying to prevent him from knocking her out and catching a case.

"I ain't going no where! Fuck this racist ass bitch!" He yelled.

"Please, baby." She begged. "Let me handle this."

He reluctantly agreed before looking at the bitter old woman once more, and going out the door.

"Mrs. Clarke--."

"I don't want to hear it!" She interrupted, waving her hands. "I want you and your kids out by morning."

Paige's eyes widened. "Mrs. Clarke, please! I just lost my job today. Where am I gonna go?" She begged.

"Oh...you lost your job too?" She laughed. "You can't do nothing right. Well it don't matter if I throw you out today or tomorrow, now does it? You eventually gonna have to get out anyway since you can't pay rent."

"But I'm paid up until the end of the week." Paige remembered.

"Well I guess you gotta be out at that time because I won't be renewing your lease." She walked to her room and slammed the door behind her.

Paige fell where she was and sobbed uncontrollably.

CHAPTER THREE

PAIGE

Having drunk a half of bottle of Hennessey, all of Tone's anger was pointed toward the door. Every vein in his body pulsed with blood and alcohol and he wanted to take it out on the woman he thought deserved it all...Paige.

After all, the old woman she rented from really outdid her self when she had a friend run his license plate only to learn he was married. The bitter broad thought it would be cute to contact Tone's wife and tell her how he jumped in an old woman's face and when that didn't get her blood boiling she told her about his infidelities.

Two months later she left Tone and although he moved in Paige, he was livid that his marriage ended and believed he made a mistake. That was one year ago to the day.

"Open this fucking door, bitch!" His forehead rested on the cool wood. "Let me hit you...I mean talk to you for a minute." He laughed to himself and took another swig of Hennessey, running one hand down the paneling.

"Please, baby! Please don't do this to me!" Paige pleaded. "I'm sorry for whatever I did, I just can't take anymore pain."

"I said, open this fucking door!"

"Okay...if I open it..." She paused, realizing he could kick it in if he wanted. "Are you gonna hit me again?"

"I can assure you, Paige Lewis, you won't be getting anything you don't deserve." He laughed hysterically. "Now open the door. Don't make me ask you again."

Paige was contemplating leaving the confines of the bathroom but with Tone nothing was certain, including her safety. She was still trying to understand how all of this happened. One moment they were making love and the next when she commented about him calling her his wife's name, he used it as an excuse to punish her. It was clear that he enjoyed abuse, often getting a sexual rise out of it.

She looked at the pink plush carpet she'd sat on for the past hour and realized she was paralyzed with fear. After all, what would she gain by stepping out? Tone's abusiveness? *Why am I here? Why is my life continually turning for the worst? What am I doing so wrong that I can't put my trust in a man and have it returned?*

Using the sink to stand up, she looked at herself in the mirror. Her face was already swollen and battered causing her to look nothing like herself. Some bruises old...some fresh. Her lip was busted and her eye was blackened from last week's tirades.

Bitterness was causing her to hate men and the games they played. What if the shoes were on the other foot? What if she was the one who beat him when she felt the weight of the world on her shoulders? Maybe then he'd understand how she felt.

She couldn't believe she'd agreed to move in with Tone a year ago after Mrs. Clarke threw her and her children out on the streets. She started not to accept his offer, but he begged saying it was best for all of them. *I love you baby.* He told her. *Why would I want to see you out on the streets? Why would I want to see you hurt? Trust me when I say my wife leaving was the best thing that ever happened to me. The best thing that happened to us.*

Since he had his own place, she agreed not wanting her kids to be without. She figured if nothing else, her children deserved a chance, maybe even a father figure. But after he beat her for six months out of the year she wished she never put her children in the predicament they were now in.

Opening up the door slightly, she was snatched out and met with another bout of rippling pain and a flood of stars. He hit her in the left eye knocking her to the floor. Dragging her by her shoulder length brown hair, he kicked her uncontrollably in the stomach before taking her in the bedroom. She would try to scream but his kicks prevented the sound from making its way out. His powerful blows pummeled her around and she even received a few blows to her breasts.

He was merciless.

"I told you not to make me mad!" He yelled. "And what do you do? Question me when I accidently call you

Courtney's name! I own you! Do you hear me? I fucking own you and can say and do what I want!"

"You're right, Tone," she coughed as her own blood filled her mouth. "I'm sorry. I'm so sorry." She paused. "I can leave if you want and stay with my friend."

"What friend?" He frowned. "You ain't got no damn friends! I'm the only friend you have and need. Don't you ever forget that."

When he saw the kids peeking into their bedroom he grew angrier. With a fist full of their mother's hair, his other hand gripped in a fist preparing to strike her bloody face he yelled, "Go back into the room! Now!"

"No…leave my mommy alone!" Marco screamed.

"Yeah, get off of her!" Marcus added before he and his brother ran toward him.

Seeing their mother balled up on the floor in pain, they refused to leave and started hitting Tone with tiny fists throughout his body. Their blows landed on his unremorseful flesh and did nothing but irritate him even more. Eventually he threw them off, slamming them against the TV.

When he had them out the way, he snatched them up, one under each underarm and rushed them to their room. All he wanted to do was take out his insecurities on Paige and nothing would stop him. Whenever something was bothering him he beat Paige. Whenever he cheated and worried she may be cheating too, he beat her. He beat her for sport and still she proved her loyalty.

That was before he laid hands on her children, something he'd never done.

When he put the kids in their room, he walked back toward his bedroom but saw Paige wasn't there. *Where in the fuck is she?* He thought. He looked in the bathroom, under the bed and in the closet and still he couldn't find her. His five-bedroom home was big, but he didn't understand how he could have missed her. Was he so fueled with hate and alcohol that he was losing his mind? And when he walked back toward the children's room, the kids weren't there either. It was then that he saw their figures hurrying toward the front door.

His hands crawled into fists. "Where do you think you're going, bitch?" He yelled running toward them.

"Just let me leave." She cried hunched over barely able to move. "You can have everything we own just let us go. Please, Tone," she cried. "You've taken so much from us all ready. All I want is my boys."

At that moment the twins cried too.

But their cries landed on deaf ears. His rage had overpowered him so much that he was unreasonable. Besides, if she left who would he beat? He ran after her to prevent her from escaping. When he reached them and grabbed her hair, he didn't see the blade she had in her hand. Paige was able to pick up the switchblade she carried in her purse for protection with all intentions on using it.

She stabbed him in the side so hard, that the handle touched his skin. There was no use in using the weapon if the goal was not severe damage, and she succeeded. With him down she gathered her boys and made the exit. She never stopped to see if he was on their heels.

She vowed never to play victim to a man again and she meant it too.

CHAPTER FOUR

PAIGE

Paige was growing irritated with the cashier at the carry out she always went to on Bladensburg Road. *Why do I even come to this mothafucka?* She always ordered the same meal for her and her kids and didn't understand why the owner insisted on getting it incorrect every time. At the same time, Paige was trying to practice a little restraint. Because she knew if she got her too upset, the woman would wipe her ass with their food or some other nasty shit.

"Ma'am...I said, twelve wings, a large fry and three grape sodas," Paige said calmly.

"Okay. You say, a twelve wing, a large fry and three grape soda?"

"Yes!"

"Okay. No reason to get hostile!" The Chinese lady said. "I just asking. I just asking!"

By Sante' Porter

"Whatever. Just bring my food please. My babies are hungry and waiting on me in the car."

"I'm moving as fast as I can. But you must wait and don't be rude!"

Paige slammed her hand on the counter. "Just bring my food!"

When the lady left, a younger Chinese lady approached the counter. She always apologized for her mother's rudeness whenever she was there. Paige preferred when she took her order instead of her mother because she understood English and was always polite. The first thing she did when her mother was out of sight was smile and shake her head. In private she warned her mother that they would lose customers if she didn't check her attitude at the door. But her mother reminded her that as mad as niggers got about her behavior, they still bought fast food so she'd always be in business.

"I'm so sorry. Please forgive my mother." She laughed. "I'll take the soda's off the tab so don't worry about it."

"Thank you." Paige smiled. "What is your name anyway?"

"Jasmine."

"Well I appreciate it, Jasmine. You're always so sweet when I come in here."

"You're a good customer. I'm supposed to be."

"Well I wish your mother felt the same way too." Paige laughed.

"She'll get it when everybody starts leaving and going down the street."

"You think that will really happen?" Paige joked.

"I don't know. I mean, mamma mean's well, but she doesn't understand that customer's make the business. She treats me bad and I am her daughter."

"Really?"

"Yes!" Jasmine laughed. "So don't feel bad. She does it to everybody, even her own husband."

Five minutes later the food arrived and Paige thanked Jasmine again and walked back toward the car but she almost passed out when she saw police officers surrounding

By Sante' Porter

it. *What's going on?* She thought. *Is something wrong?* She felt panicky. She dropped the food when she saw her kids where in the officer's custody. She ran toward them but she couldn't seem to reach them fast enough.

"Can I help you?" Paige asked out of breath. "Why do you have my fucking kids?"

"Are you Paige Lewis?" The black lady asked who was not in a police uniform. "Ma'am! Are you Paige Lewis?"

"Yes...I am and these are my twin boys." Paige was talking but she didn't understand how it was possible seeing as though she could barely catch her breath. Her world was coming to an official end.

"Well...I'm Bridget Saratoga from The Department of Social Services."

Paige didn't care who she was. All she knew was that she was the most frightening person she'd ever seen in her life. Standing before her, in a black on black pants suit with her hair pulled back in a bun, the officer was taking what was left of her life.

"Why would you leave your children alone?" Bridget asked, in a condescending and unsympathetic tone.

"I...didn't...I."

Bridget cut her off and said, "It doesn't matter and we're taking them into our custody now."

"I don't understand why you're taking my fucking kids?" Paige shot back after seeing her boys being taken inside of one of the cars.

"Mommy, please! Don't let them take us."

"Ma'am, please! Don't do this," Paige said as she moved toward the car before one of the two uniformed officers could restrain her.

"There's no use in you acting up. Don't let your children see you behaving this way. You've done enough harm."

"But why is this happening?" Paige cried as her tears fell into her words like buckets of water. "I'm confused! It doesn't make any sense."

"For starters, we've received several reports that you may be living in your car and that you're an unfit mother.

We've also received a report that your children aren't even going to school. Is that true?"

Paige couldn't stop to think about who could have made up such a vicious lie; all she wanted were her kids. But she had a feeling it was Tone. She felt she didn't have to answer to anyone because rain or shine, she *always* got her children up from the back seat of the car, took them to IHOP to wash their faces and bodies as best as they could, and took them to school. This was now her full time job.

"Ma'am...is it true?"

Paige didn't answer due to focusing on her children's mute cries from behind the window in the closed police car.

"Okay...By what we can see...and judging by the questions we've just asked your children, we've determined that it is true. So until you can find appropriate housing for them, they'll be wards of the state of Maryland."

"Miss..." Paige said slowly. "You can't take my kids. I'll die without my kids. Do you hear me? I'll die without my boys."

"For your sake and theirs I hope not." She said while getting into the car. "Otherwise, how will you get your children back?"

Paige fell to the ground and cried uncontrollably. She remained there until Jasmine came running outside to comfort her. And for that moment, Jasmine saved her, because she had all intentions of not living.

By Sante' Porter

CHAPTER FIVE
SIX MONTHS LATER
PUSH

Push decided to go to Tonio's crib to cut the work in the trunk of his car. Ordinarily he would have a worker care for it but time was not on his side so the job needed to be done by himself. A few New York niggas were on their way down and he needed business handled like yesterday.

In one aspect he had everything going good in his world. It wasn't farfetched to say that he and his boys were self-made millionaires, kings in the drug business. And yet he fucked a girl who got pregnant and now lived with her although he despised her, believing she trapped him.

He was driving down New York Avenue when he passed the most beautiful woman he'd ever seen in his life. She wasn't ordinary and he had to have her. He never saw a female as bad as her before. Her hair rested on the red sweater she was wearing and she sported a pair of jeans so form fitting, he thanked God twice for looking out.

Double-parking his white 2015 Mercedes Benz on the side of the road, he jumped out to get her attention. He wondered why she was walking until he saw she was going toward a strip club during day hours. She was startled when he tapped her shoulder and he could tell she was about to let him have a piece of her mind, until she looked into his eyes.

Push was fine and his looks shocked her. He had to be no good.

"Yes. Can I help you?" she held her purse against her chest and crossed over it.

"Name?" Push went in.

"Excuse me?"

"I need to know your name so I can know what to call my future wife."

She laughed. And when she did he knew he had her.

"My name's Paige and you need to get rid of that line. I've heard it before." She was hesitant. Men hurt her before and she had to be careful on who she trusted. "But I have to go. I'm sorry."

"Paige and Push. I like the sound of that. You single?"

"No!" she yelled approaching the door.

"I don't care about that nigga anyway."

She giggled.

"You dance here? Because if you do it won't be for long."

She laughed.

He moved closer. "You gonna be mine and I'll be here everyday until I prove my point."

She giggled again.

That woman is made for me.

He thought.

Little did he know, beginning this very moment, he was in for the ride of his life.

As promised, Push was parked right at the corner the next day waiting for Paige. She knew he was there before she saw his face because his music was pumping. But today she didn't feel like entertaining because losing her kids wore down on her even more. She was nowhere near getting them back and she finally understood they might be lost in the system forever. She also learned that Tone was to blame for losing the twins when he told authorities that she stabbed him, leaving out the reason why. They couldn't pen a case on her without sufficient evidence but they could keep her kids. To top it all off she still didn't have a steady job.

Outside of fucking a few dudes who didn't want to commit, she didn't have a man either.

Upset thinking about her babies and not in the mood to kick it, Paige rushed past Push's car to try and ease inside the building unnoticed. But Push had been waiting, so he saw her and her tears.

"Paige...what's wrong with you?" he jumped out of his ride and blocked her path.

"Just leave me alone please!" She waved him off.

"I'm not gonna leave you alone." He rested his hands on her shoulders and it comforted her immediately. She felt safe in his presence.

"Now what's going on and don't say nothing?" He continued. "Are you hurt?"

"It's my kids!" she sighed. "Something happened and I haven't seen them in a while.

"Why not?"

"A long story."

Push was interested but at the same time he wasn't a social worker. He didn't know what to say because truthfully he had a kid on the way by a bitch in his house that he wasn't feeling. So more kids weren't on the menu.

"If you not gonna talk, let me get you something to eat. Or better yet, get some drinks. And we can kick it about anything you want." He paused. "Come on, cutie. Let me make you smile."

And when Push felt he was breaking her down he said, "*Henny* on the rocks will do the trick. You won't think about your problems for the rest of the night. I promise."

Then she really looked at him. This was the kind of nigga who could send her to the crazy house for years. "I can't do this right now." She cried running into the building. "I just can't."

Paige had been thinking about the stranger all day and wondered if he wasn't the answer to her prayers. After all, she'd been asking hard for someone to be in her life. A man she could talk to. His kindness despite, how rude she was, made her like him.

A lot.

Her problem was that the last time she allowed a guy to invade her soul she ended up plunging metal into his body just to get away from him. To this day she doesn't know if he was trying to hunt her down now.

Thinking about Tone caused her discomfort but she shook it off feeling justified in her actions remembering how he manhandled her boys. She vowed that if he came for her she would do it again, in a heartbeat.

By Sante' Porter

Still, she couldn't help but wonder how things would've been if she decided to jump into Push's car. But she wouldn't have to guess for long.

When she came out of the club, after cleaning it, since her stripper days were long over, she heard music and smiled when his Benz came into view. She walked up to it and looked through the passenger side window.

"What are you doing here?" she smiled trying to hide her excitement. "I don't recall giving you and invite."

"I figured I'd speed things up since you gonna end up being my wife anyway. So you gonna stop playing games and roll with me or nah?"

"I don't know."

"Okay how 'bout this. I'ma ask you four questions that you gotta be real about. If you say yes to any one of 'em, you coming with me."

She nodded.

"Are you feeling me?"

"Yes."

"Are you tired of being by yourself?"

"Yes."

"Were you thinking about me before I popped up?" She hid her smile and he pushed the door open to his car. "Get inside, shawty. Let's start the rest of our lives now. We wasting too much time."

She looked around to be sure nobody saw her. And suddenly not caring anymore if they did she eased in. "I gotta ask you three questions now," she said.

"Go." He leaned back in his seat thinking she was cute.

"Are you feeling me?"

"Yes."

"Are you single?"

He thought it best to lie. "Yeah."

"Do you want a serious relationship? Somebody who will be in your corner and who would never leave you because she doesn't want to be alone herself?"

Push's dick got hard because he felt he was finally in there until she raised her hand. "Before you answer I gotta say this...don't lie to me, Push. Whatever you do, please don't lie."

He had intentions on telling her whatever she wanted to hear. He was all about the fast forward option and his focus was clear. "I want somebody to be with that I can look out for on an exclusive tip. Maybe it's you."

"Then let's make it official," she said. "Kiss me."

"Official?" He repeated. Everything in his spirit said to go the other way...right now.

"Yes, if you want me and I want you, let's make it official with a kiss."

He felt she was moving way too fast but he knew after it was all said and done he could get rid of her if she did too much. He already had one crazy chick at home and wasn't trying to have another. Still, he threw all caution out the window and leaned until he touched her lips.

It was a long kiss, one full of passion and he found himself wanting to have her immediately. After the kiss was over she said, "That was good, now you're mine."

CHAPTER SIX

PUSH

For a month Push had been keeping time with Paige and for real things were running smoothly, except for one thing, he was in a relationship already. He knew Lala would not take the news well but Paige was everything he dreamed of in a wifey. She kept a clean apartment, even though it was small. She fucked him right and she knew how to make him feel. He feared if he didn't exile his live in girlfriend, and soon, Paige would leave him.

He walked through the door of his modest house in Washington DC and threw a sack of money on the table. As usual the house stunk like shit and there was no food cooking.

He stood at the bottom of the steps. "Lala! Get out here, man! We gotta talk now!

A minute later she came down, rubbing her eyes. "What's going on?"

"I'm 'bout to tell you."

She walked down the steps, stroking her six-month pregnant belly.

"Is everything cool?"

"You gotta pack all your shit and move back to your own crib, shawty," Push said getting straight to the point. "I want you gone today. Don't let the nightfall catch your ass still in my crib."

Her jaw dropped and tears rolled down her cheeks. She knew this moment would come since he'd been out the house a lot but she hadn't expected him to go hard so soon. He acted like he didn't even know her, like she was a bum broad off the street instead of housing his baby in her body.

"Push, you playing right? I'm gonna clean up if that's a problem."

"It ain't about that no more. We off that shit now."

She looked around and started picking up jeans, t-shirts and all kinds of other things that she left around when she thought he wouldn't care. The truth was Push was gone so much that she started to treat the house like it was her own.

She didn't clean up at her own place and she didn't clean up at his. It didn't bother him before because her fuck game deserved a medal but that all changed. Paige was now in the picture and he felt she was official.

"Push, I'm not leaving here without at least fighting for my man."

When she started crying heavily he felt a little something for the kid. He was a thorough nigga but it was difficult for him to look at her so he walked toward the kitchen to avoid the scene.

It didn't stop the emotions from falling. Lala started sobbing uncontrollably when he walked off. "But, but, what am I going to do?"

"You act like you don't have a place of your own."

"But I want to be here, Push! With you!"

"Come here," Push said in a cool and calm manner. He sat on the chair by the dining table.

Lala ran, not walked, toward him. She dropped to her knees and he looked down on her as if he were her savior and in control of her life.

By Sante' Porter

"What did I do, Push?" she cried. "Tell me. Is it because I keep going through your phone? Or calling you during meetings?"

He wiped her tears away with his thumb. "Stop crying," he said softly. "Now I care about you. Was even feeling you at one point but we were moving so fast that we got caught up in the family game and it ain't for me. I have to go on with my life but I want you to know I'ma do good by the kid. I put that on the dope game."

Lala looked at him and touched his hand. "Push, aren't you happy with me anymore? If you not what can I do to make things right?" she wiped tears away. "And prove that I love you and I always will? I'm willing to do anything."

He looked into her eyes. At one point she was his rock. His soldier. He provided everything she needed because she took care of him. And now he saw her as another obstacle in the way of being with Paige. And that was a major problem.

"It just ain't working. It be like that sometimes." He shrugged. "Now I'll help you move back to your apartment but you got to go."

"Yo Tonio talking too much lately, Push," Orlando said as he and Push walked ahead of Tonio and Mick at the Boulevard. Orlando was a yellow nigga with a mole under his right eye and a serious bop to his step. But he was also loyal to Push and kept him abreast of all danger. They were on their way to get new kicks. "He letting niggas know how we get our money and what not. Talking about how you don't even fuck with DC niggas no more since the New York connect came through."

Push could feel his temperature rise as he listened to the word. "How you know for sure?"

"Tonio told me himself how he be putting it to these other niggas. And how niggas is mad because they don't make the paper we do." He paused. "He dangerous, dog. You have to get this situation together."

Push was quiet because he also noticed Tonio had a mouthpiece on him. The only reason he didn't deal with it

By Sante' Porter

earlier was that he was hoping with time it would go away. Plus Tonio was his man, and he couldn't push off on him like he would do someone else.

He was wrong.

"Oh, and I heard you got another chick," Orlando said. Now he was the one with bitch teeth. "Some girl name Paige."

"And how you know that?" Push frowned.

Orlando laughed. "How you think? Your man told me that too."

Something was going to have to give. Push just needed time to think.

"Thanks for letting me know, fam."

"No doubt," he said giving him a pound. "I been trying to tell you all day, but Tonio be on you like a leech, playing you close. I'm surprised he ain't run up here between us now."

Push grinned, still fucked up with the info.

They walked slowly allowing Mick and Tonio to catch up before dipping into the shoe store and pretending as if nothing happened. But Push was going to have to pull Tonio up soon before shit got out of control in his crew and on the streets.

"Yo…give me all these Jordan's…size twelve." Push told the sales person in the shoe store. He pulled out his cash and flung it on the counter. "And throw in a couple packs of them Nike socks."

There were a bunch of Thirsty Thots inside of the store hoping to be seen by Push and his team. Although they would've settled for either one of the fellas, they really wanted Push because he seemed to have the money, power and respect.

"Save some shit for me to buy," Tonio said as he bought a few boxes of shoes himself. "You taking up all the good shit."

By the time they left, they were loaded to the head.

"So what you 'bout to do now?" Tonio asked Push as he wrestled with his bags.

"Nothing." His tone was flat, still mad about what Orlando told him.

"Well it looks like you 'bout to get in with shawty," Tonio said, pointing at Paige who was walking in his direction.

Although it was a surprise, she looked beyond sexy. Her bob haircut hung on her shoulders and her jeans were tight enough to confirm that all curves were in place. The fellas seemed pleasantly surprised loving the eye candy for the moment.

Paige walked up to him and kissed him on the lips. "Hey, baby."

He grinned since all eyes gave him the nod of approval. "What you doing here?"

"I saw your car in the parking lot and came through." She grabbed his hand. "Wanted to escort you home for dinner."

When he looked over her head, his friends, who were behind her, were trying to hide their laughter. She was playing him closer than he wanted anybody to see. They didn't know the relationship got this serious. "Oh, well I was about to get with them for a few more ticks. I'll be home afterwards."

She looked behind her and saw Tonio laughing the hardest and because of it she hated him the most.

"No," she shook her head. "You will be home now."

"But I'm with my dudes."

"They're more important than me?"

Push really felt put on the spot now. "They are important and I'll get at you when I'm done."

She rolled her eyes. "Well I made dinner already." She looked at the gold Bulova watch he bought her on her wrist. "Besides, you were due home five minutes ago. If you ask me, you're already done." She pulled him towards the parking lot, the sounds of his friend's laughter trailed off behind him."

By Sante' Porter

CHAPTER SEVEN

PUSH

Push was in bed after eating a large meal at Paige's place. He'd been quiet all night because although he was feeling her, he didn't appreciate her possessiveness or the scene. He was a drug dealer and dope boys needed their space. Which she obviously wasn't trying to provide.

They went to bed, without saying much to each other. For real the only thing he mouthed was that tomorrow, after his hearing for parking ticket violations, they had to have a conversation. Paige was still consumed with thoughts about her kids so she didn't notice that he was angry with her. Her mood dipped up and down when she thought about him. It was pitch dark in her room when Push felt the covers pull back from his body and the cool air rush over him due to the air condition being on blast.

"Paige, what you doing?" he asked looking at the red glare from the clock radio. "It's four in the morning and I got to go to court in a few hours. I told you that."

"You know what I'm doing, Push." She kissed his lips, sucking the bottom one really hard. "Now stop playing with me and come get this pussy."

"Paige...I don't feel like doing this right now. Besides, we got to talk later about some things.

"We can talk about everything you want right now while your dick is in my mouth." She rustled with his boxers, wanting nothing more than to fuck to get her problems off her mind.

"Have you been paying attention? I've been fucked up with you all night." He stated as he grabbed her wrists and held them firmly in his hands. "And you not in control of this thing, I am!"

"Fuck that shit!" she said getting louder. "You here, in my bed. What you think we gonna do except fuck?" She frowned. "Now stop playing and make love to me, please."

She was crazy...out of her mind. But the mere fact that she was begging him turned Push on.

"Paige, I hope I ain't make a mistake!" he continued, now kissing her gently. His body was doing the exact opposite of what his mouth was saying. "I'm..."

"You're my man." She continued as she slid her slippery wetness onto the tip of his dick. "And I'm gonna do whatever I want to you."

One thing for sure, the bitch was about her business in the bedroom. She bucked her hips with the moves of a professional. "You gonna have to give me some space if we gonna do this relationship thing."

"I know, baby, I know. Just remember that I own you."

"Why you keep saying that shit?" he yelled lifting her up off him. He paced the room with his dick rock hard and sticking out of his boxers. "I ain't 'bout to be with nobody who gonna be popping up on me and shit! You hear me? I can't! As a matter of fact I'm about to bounce."

"Please don't go, Push." Her knees hit the floor as she put his dick into her mouth. She wanted to catch his thickness before it went back down so she continued to get to business. "I just want to be everything to you. I promise, I won't be so bossy anymore." She uttered around the hard penis resting in her mouth.

Her tongue moved ferociously over his dick and she could taste her bittersweet wetness mixed with his juices. There was no way he could handle her need to taste him. "Ahhhhh... shit," he cried out as his head fell against the wall, before he looked back down at her. "You feel so fucking good!"

Before he knew it, she stood up, bent down in front of him and wiggled her dripping wet pussy onto his dick again. He was no match for Paige who knew what she wanted. His hands held the sides of her waist as he looked down at her fat ass jiggling and bouncing on his dick.

"You like that shit don't you? Tell me how much you like it. Tell me that you're mine." She demanded.

He was silent as he came to terms that something about her would not let him leave. She had him just where she wanted him, in all senses.

"I know you love it, Push." She continued backing against him harder, squeezing her inner walls each time.

By Sante' Porter

"Bust that nut into this pussy. Cum hard for me, daddy. I wanna feel that shit."

She didn't have to say another word. "I'm about to cuuummm!" He yelled out. "Fuck!" He moaned as he released himself inside of her holding her hips in place.

When he was done she stood up and kissed him. "Now what did you want to talk about?" She kissed his chin, thinking it was funny. "What did you want to tell me that was so important?"

He looked into her eyes. "I put my girl out yesterday, if you want you can move in with me."

She winked. "Of course I do." Then she dropped to her knees and licked him clean.

Again.

Push was sitting in Paige's small living room, talking to Orlando on the phone. One of their trap houses had been robbed and Orlando believed it was a result of Tonio bumping his gums again on the block.

"So what you want me to do, man?" Orlando asked.

Push rubbed is throbbing temples. First he had his big mouth friend to deal with then there was Paige, who after a morning of amazing sex, he told could live with him. "Don't do anything, I'll handle it." He ended the call.

"Handle what?" Paige asked stepping into the living room.

"Sorry, babe, didn't mean to wake you."

"You didn't wake me. I'm just up to make breakfast for your hospitality." As she walked over to the refrigerator Push watched her ass that jiggled under her boy shorts. Pulling the fridge's door open she said, "So what's wrong?"

"Nothing, just Tonio."

"Please say he didn't do it."

His eyes widened and he stood up. "Do what?"

"Oh, it's nothing." She grabbed the eggs, salsa and bacon and placed it on the counter, before closing the fridge's door.

"Do what?" He yelled.

"I overheard at the strip club that he was gonna have you robbed. Something about not trusting you for dealing with New York niggas now." Paige was lying out her mouth but tried her hand.

With her children gone she was growing selfish, erratic and possessive and unfortunately for Push he represented home for her. And she needed her home to be safe.

Push felt gut punched. "Why didn't you tell me that before?"

"Because at the Boulevard you said your dudes were important. That was one of the reasons I got out of my car when I spotted yours and came looking for you yesterday. I wanted you to know."

Push backed up and bumped into the table. He dipped toward the bedroom. "Babe, I'll be back. I gotta go handle something right quick."

She shrugged and continued to cook. Having gotten her revenge for Tonio laughing at her never felt so good.

CHAPTER EIGHT
PUSH

Push was patient when dealing with Tonio because he wanted to be sure. But now it was time.

It was midnight when Push, with Mick and Orlando by his side, stood on the deck of the boat docks. This meeting was private and last minute but needed to be done. After having gotten the word from Orlando about the hit and then Paige, Push felt he could no longer trust Tonio.

"Push, please don't do this! You have to listen to me! It wasn't like that!"

"It wasn't like what, Tonio, clear it up for me?"

"It wasn't me who set you up and it wasn't me who hit the shop! You know I'd never do that." His face was wet with tears and that enraged Push because he knew he was responsible. "Please, let's at least talk about this in private. You gotta hear my side of this shit!"

"It's nothing else to talk about, fam. You fucked up. Had

By Sante' Porter

it not been for me finding out early, my other houses could've been hit. You running around town telling niggas how we get our money and 'bout business that don't have shit to do with you! Why shouldn't I drop yo ass, Tonio?"

What Orlando and Mick didn't know was that Push wanted him to say something, just one thing to convince him to spare his life. He was the one dude Push knew would bend over backwards for him, but his chatter game was too strong and Push hated that trait about him.

"'Cause you know me that's why, Push."

"You ain't said nothing worth hearing yet, nigga "

Push cocked his gun.

"Okay...okay. Uh...I don't know who robbed the spot but I, um, I think it may have been Lala's brother."

"Lala's brother?" Push looked at him and then Orlando and Mick. "What you talking about?" He frowned.

"I don't have all the details but I know he was mad at how you did her, by throwing her out while she knocked up with your kid."

"Fuck this nigga talking 'bout? Put it too his ass, Push." Mick interrupted. "What you waiting on?"

"Man I'm giving you a chance to tell me why I should spare your fucking life and you rapping to me about Lala and her brother? You betta come with something else, bruh. The clock is ticking!"

"It's all I know! If it was something else I'd say it and you wouldn't have to do this either."

"Push, don't listen to this shit. Scared niggas got no heart and they lie," Mick interjected.

Push looked at Mick and Orlando and they both shrugged their shoulders. Even if it were true, would it be enough to save his life? It could be a reason to kill him anyway, considering he waited until his deathbed to tell him.

Push decided then that he didn't believe him. For real he didn't want to believe him. "You got one more chance to convince me, Tonio. Just one!"

Tonio was silent before talking, knowing this would be his last chance. "You should let me live because we family.

And I would never hurt you. Don't nobody know all the shit we've been through, man. Don't do this. I may talk a lot but it's never to hurt you. Please."

His response tugged at Push's heart a little, but his words were also *too* soft to be taken seriously especially in front of the men. In the end Tonio failed and it was his fault.

"Not good enough, Tonio." He told him coldly. He looked at Orlando. "Off him and dump him in the river."

"Please don't do this!"

Tonio's pleas were hard for Push to hear but the order was given and Orlando approached him.

"Push, please!" Tonio screamed. "At least let my mother find my body! Let her give me a proper funeral! You treating me like we not even boys!"

Not wasting time, Mick grabbed Tonio's right arm while Orlando stood over him with the gun to his dome. Orlando looked at Push once more before Push nodded. The gun sounded off and Tonio's body was tossed in the river.

CHAPTER NINE
TWO MONTHS LATER
PAIGE

Paige sat in her car, frustrated about missing her appointment with Bridget Saratoga from The Department of Social Services about the twins. Paige was scheduled for a visit earlier to see what needed to be done to get her children back but she preferred to meet away from their house. Besides, since Push was making more money in the dope game they were living like rock stars in what resembled a mansion. Paige was afraid that would raise additional questions causing Push's dope game to be exposed.

She went to clean her old apartment that Push still paid the rent on, but when she was done too much time had passed. When her phone rang she grabbed it with and attitude. "Hello!"

By Sante' Porter

"Paige, this is Bridget Saratoga. I'm returning your call but is this a bad time?"

She straight threw on her professional voice and said, "Oh...uh...no. I thought you were somebody playing on my phone but I can definitely talk now."

"I see...can you bring the volume down on your music in the background? I can barely hear you."

Paige hadn't realized it was on because her thoughts were swirling. She quickly adjusted the sound. "I'm sorry. Thanks for returning my call."

"Well, I must say, it didn't look good that you missed your appointment today. I mean do you want your children back or not?"

"Yes, ma'am. Of course I do!"

"Well right now I'm not sure what's going to happen. You're coming across as very unprofessional and unreliable. I must say it's not a good look. If you miss one more appointment I don't know if we'll be able to reunite you with your family."

"But they are my kids!"

"Ma'am, I've seen enough children in this system to know when they aren't being cared for and you certainly dropped the ball. Therefore we have scheduled an appointment with you on Monday of next week to follow up. We will have to discuss it further at that time."

"Ma'am, there's been a mistake on how you perceive me. I really am a good parent and Tone lied to you because he was beating me and I told."

The woman sighed, not believing her. "We'll see about that when we meet again, Paige. You'll also have to submit to testing for yourself."

Paige adjusted in her seat. Since most of her time was spent on obsessing over Push, she used weed to calm her nerves. She used it so much she couldn't sleep without it. "That won't be a problem. But where are they right now? I been calling all over and nobody seems to know nothing."

"I'll get to that in a minute, Paige," she paused. "We are gonna also need you to bring proof of employment when you come to the office so that we can make an evaluation, that is, in the event things work out for you."

By Sante' Porter

She was making Paige's blood boil by threatening the reunion with her kids. "I got all that, but can you tell me where they have my children placed?"

"They are," Bridget paused and she heard papers shuffling in the background, "Let's see...in a foster home in Bladensburg Maryland. They're staying with a nice family who owns a Chinese food restaurant. They are doing well and as of now are still together."

Paige sat up. "Wait, is there someone named Jasmine living in the home?"

"As a matter of fact, yes." She paused. "Now if everything is in order after my evaluation, your kids can come back. Just remember to bring the documentation that we need and stay out of trouble. Can you do that, Ms. Lewis?"

"Yeah, I should be able to do that." She rolled her eyes.

"By the way, how *are* you supporting yourself these days?"

"Uh...I...uh...have a job."

"Well it's very important that we can verify that as well. After leaving the kids in the car you better be lucky you aren't going to jail."

Paige rolled her eyes. "Okay, ma'am."

"I hope you have a nice day and that you live up to your promises." She paused. "Or you can lose them for good."

When the call was over Paige tossed the cell phone in the passenger seat and thought about everything she said. She picked up the phone several times to call Push but she couldn't get through to him.

Although the money he made was good, she also bared witness to how much he changed. At one point he was always up her ass and the next thing she knew he never had the time. The streets were calling, he told her repeatedly. Something told her that he was up to no good. But first she had to visit Jasmine at that Chinese food spot and see what was up with her children.

CHAPTER TEN

PAIGE

Paige rushed home after checking the Chinese food spot where Jasmine worked but she wasn't there. She decided to try later when she got more time. Having to go to the bathroom she hit it to her house and parked in the back since it was closer to the basement and the bathroom on the lower level. When she finished she realized the toilet wouldn't flush.

She walked out, about to tell Push, when she heard, "Damn your pussy wet as shit, girl. What you doing to me?"

Was Paige hearing things correctly? Was she losing what was left of her mind? With everything she was going through it was certainly possible. Slowly she opened the door to the bedroom across the way and saw white sheets moving up and down. Two bodies were obviously there.

Suddenly the sheet fell down and the muscles in Push's back flexed with each thrust. "Push? What the fuck is going on?" She walked further into the room and stopped, waiting for an answer that made sense.

He jumped up from the bed snatching the sheets off the whore who lived down the block to cover his body. "Oh shit, babe! What you doing here? I thought you had that visit for the kids. Did it go okay?"

"I fucking live here, Push! Remember!" Paige rarely yelled but now seemed fitting. "How could you do this to me when you promised you would never break my heart?" she sobbed. "You just like the rest of them niggas aren't you?"

"I'm sorry, Paige!" the neighbor said covering her sweat soaked body with her hands. "It was just the one time!"

"Bitch, shut the fuck up!" she yelled pointing at her. "If I thought you were worth it I'd scratch your fucking eyes out your head but I'm not into wasting my time."

Paige stumbled backwards and the wall caught her limp body before it hit the floor. She was done with this nigga. She had her kids to think about and once again another man played her like a fool.

She heard Push's voice trailing off behind her as she ran out the door and into her Acura. If he wanted whores, fuck him! She was better than the nigga anyway.

If only she could stop crying.

Paige went from bad to worse when her only friend in the world, Asia was killed in a car accident. After the tragedy, it didn't take Paige long before she was back under Push's spell. The funeral took every ounce of strength she could muster and she needed him. He begged and pleaded with her to come back to him and loneliness made her his victim.

"I'm gonna take you some place you've never been before," he told her with tears in his eyes as he begged for forgiveness. "You'll see, everything's gonna be perfect."

Paige sat nervously in the airport as he held her hand. "You aight, babe?" he said softly.

"I'm fine, Push." Her voice low and unsure. "You just broke my heart and you said you wouldn't. That's just hard to forgive so forgive me if things aren't the same right away."

"I know, but I'm gonna make it up to you." He paused. "You trust me right?"

"Yeah. I just don't trust myself because with everything I got going on I can't deal with this. I feel unsafe with you and I want to be safe. More than anything."

"Let's not worry about the details of what happened right now. Let's just be together."

Once she boarded the plane heading to Mexico, Paige was becoming excited. Suddenly she had forgotten about everything she'd seen in the basement. It was as if what she saw didn't exist. Push filled something in her heart that she longed for and she wanted to hold on to it for as long as possible. Even if it wasn't real.

When they landed they jumped into a beautiful limo and headed to the Fiesta Americana Grand Coral Beach. Push rented a suite for a couple of nights just to get away. The moment they opened the door she saw beautiful long stemmed red roses and a large dish of white chocolate covered strawberries on the table. The large window was open and overlooked the beach and the scene stole her breath.

"This is beautiful, Push." She looked out the window. He pulled up two chairs for them to sit down in and enjoy the view and for a second she stared at him.

"I made a mistake and I wanted to show you the man I can be, Paige. Niggas make mistakes and I'm one of them."

She looked down at him. "Who are you? Really? Because I want to let go but I don't know."

"I'm just a man, feeling a woman." He paused. "I'm just a man who made mistakes."

"I'm so scared."

"Paige, I don't want you thinking about what happened back there. We in Mexico, in the perfect place to start all over. I ain't bring you out here just to fuck. I mean if you want to we can definitely get busy but it's not like that today."

She laughed. "Then what is it like?"

He dipped into his pocket and pulled out a red velvet box. Paige felt faint but she maintained her stance. She covered her mouth with her trembling hands. Was this the man her mother told her about? "Push, please..."

He touched her to calm down and got on one knee. "Paige, I'm really feeling you." He reassured. "And right now, I got a lot going on around me, and being with you is the only time I'm not tripping off of that shit. You're my soldier and I need you in my life."

"I feel the same, Push." Tears rolled down her face.

"So will you do me the honor of being my wife?"

"Of course, I will, Push." He slid the ring on her finger and she jumped up and hugged him. "Of course I will be your wife!"

They talked for hours about their future life and dreams. He asked more about her kids, which is something he never did. He told her he'd do whatever to help her get them back and she cried in his arms as he kissed her tears away. Push made her feel strong when she felt weak. When the night

By Sante' Porter

came they walked on the beach and made love on the sand,

with Paige excited that she would finally be someone's wife.

CHAPTER ELEVEN
TWO MONTHS LATER
PAIGE

Push, Orlando and Mick were at Twirl's strip club in DC. They had huge stacks of cash on the table in front of them and they peeled bills off based on the best female doing her thing.

Management tried everything in their power to get the girls to remain focused on *all* of the customers in the club, but it was next to impossible with Push in the building. Two strippers had already gotten into a fight trying to get Push's attention on the center stage and he ignored them both.

He liked his ladies classy.

"So you know we can't find the nigga Moats right?" Push asked as he smoked a black and mild and watched a stripper with a body like Nicki Minaj twirl on the pole. "We searched high and low and there's no haps."

"This nigga getting on my last fucking nerves." Orlando said sipping his Hennessy. "Bow out gracefully, nigga. You lost."

"Exactly. He see we ain't backing down but he don't give a fuck. He ready to die for them blocks and he gonna have to come from up under 'em."

The rest of the crew sat around them as they enjoyed the view while the bosses talked business. "He may be willing to die but I know he got a weak spot, everybody do. We just have to find it."

"I don't have one," Push offered. "Ain't nothing ever weak about me."

"You must've forgot about women."

Push laughed knowing he was right. He was a sucker for a soft pussy. "You got me on that. But I got an idea though on what we can do to get the nigga moving. I'ma send a message that he won't forget."

"You think there's anything to worry about if you make a move?"

"No, especially with us bringing the bulk of our business back to DC. Niggas not hating no more so we good."

Orlando nodded. "You still having that party for your fiancé?"

"Yeah, but she been tripping a lot lately. I need a little more space."

"So you gonna cancel her party because you being selfish?"

"Ain't saying all that. Just need some space."

Orlando nodded. "You just betta not fake. She done called my girl and got her excited about it and everything."

"I know, my only thing is there be mad pussy at that spot. I'd hate to pull something warm with Paige in the same room. She'd go ballistic."

"So don't."

"Easier said than done, nigga, you talking to me."

Orlando nodded. "True."

When a chick with a high ass and just the right sized titties came out she had Push and Orlando's attention. "She bad as fuck," Orlando said. "Damn."

"Shawty is fire. But if she ain't fucking without the 'take me out' shit I'm not for it. I need quick relief these days. Paige hawks too much to get something going long term. Fucking up a nigga's whole game."

When the girl turned around and Push saw who it was he stood up. His eyes widened. "Lala, what you doing up there?"

Embarrassed she stopped moving, opened her eyes wide and ran off the stage. "I'll be right back, O. Let me see about her." He went to the back and grabbed her up. "The fuck is you doing out there?"

"What do you want, Push?"

"How you been? This the kind of shit you been doing? Shaking your ass in a strip club for coins?"

She pulled away from him. "Don't act like you care. You moved on remember? Moved a new bitch into your new house and everything."

"It's not like that."

"Then what is it like? You don't give a fuck about me. You never have."

He sighed. "I made a mistake for treating you like that. Let me make it up to you. Can we hang out tomorrow?" He rubbed his hands together, fantasizing about her fuck game.

"This is hard for me." She cried. "Real hard, Push."

"Then say yes. Make it easy."

She looked into his eyes. "You're gonna hurt me again, I know it."

"I promise all I want to do is hang out, like old friends." He looked her over again. "You look good, real good." He paused, wondering if he should ask the next question. "Ever have the baby?"

"No, I lost it after you left me."

He felt bad but also extremely relieved. "Let me take you out, and if you don't want to have anything to do with me after that, I'll walk away for good. It's your call."

CHAPTER TWELVE

PAIGE

Tomorrow Paige had her final visit with social services to get her children back. She felt hopeful. She did everything to welcome them home including painting their rooms. If only her fiancé was as happy about his extended family as she was. Whenever she went to talk to him about it he would skip the subject and it was clear what position he stood on.

She was about to pay for her food in the grocery store when a pretty girl with a long brown weave came inside. She walked right up to her and smiled. "You don't know me but I know you very well."

Paige nodded and frowned. "That's good for you."

"I know it is. And I'm going to tell you like I told them other bitches who came before you and who will probably come after you. When it comes to Push he's gonna always love me.

Paige's stomach rumbled because not only did she not know the chick, she couldn't guess why she was approaching her when she wore the ring and lived with him. "You know what, I suggest —"

Paige's sentence was stopped when Lala who had been back in the picture for one month since he ran into her in the strip club, slapped her in the lips. They twirled around the store, knocking everything over in sight. Some how Paige managed to get on top of her and that's when she really got to wailing on her face. Before Paige knew it she was grabbed up by a police officer and taken away.

FIVE MONTHS LATER

When Paige's cell door opened, she sat up on the bunk and wiped the tears from her eyes. She was afraid she would be forced to fight again, like she had every other month, until she saw Officer Crane, a handsome guard with brown

By Sante' Porter

eyes and a wide smile. "Your commissary came in. You can go pick it up."

Paige stood up and was escorted down the hall. She received her ticket and purchased some things she needed. Mainly her toiletries like deodorant, soap and lotion. Snacks were there too but she wasn't in the mood. She lost so much weight from not eating that she could barely fit her orange jumpsuit.

When she got back to her cell she was surprised to see a letter on her bunk. She put her items up and sat down to read it:

Paige,

I know shit has been hard for you but I want you to know you got me. I'm not going anywhere. I'm forever loyal and willing to do whatever I can to prove to you that I'm down.

Keep your head up. In two more months you'll be home and I'll be waiting. I'll make it up to you, you'll see.

Your nigga, Push.

Tears rolled down her cheeks and she balled the letter up, spit on it and tossed it in the trash. She had plans for him. Sweet plans but they would all have to wait.

He didn't pick her up from jail, but then again she wasn't surprised. He said he had business and couldn't get away. He was a no account nigga for sure. The Uber pulled up to her house and all she wanted to do was get clean. It had been seven months since she took a hot shower and even longer since she had privacy.

Life had been difficult since Paige was arrested. She didn't have a job and would rely on Push for everything but Paige had plans for more.

When Paige made it to the house, she looked behind herself for strangers and lifted the flowerpot, removed the key, opened the door and let herself inside. Everything was clean and it smelled like a woman. Although the furniture

By Sante' Porter

was new before she went to jail now it seemed lived on. Pictures from the few visits of them in prison were over the living room like Push just threw them up.

Exhausted, she walked to the bedroom and sat on the edge of the bed before exhaling. Everything was neat in the room. A little too neat.

When something caught her eye on the table beside the bed, she picked it up and saw it was a letter.

Paige,

> *I had to get with my man on some business. I had a chef make you some food. I feel bad I'm not there but I'll be home soon and we'll get into something nice.*
>
> *P.S. Your meal is in the fridge.*

I can't stand this nigga. She thought.

Paige took a shower and stayed inside until the water ran cold. Afterwards she ate the lasagna in the fridge and took a nap. When she woke up two hours later Push was not home. It was cool though; she could use the extra time to perfect her plan.

Five hours later, when the moon was at it's highest, Push finally came home smelling like alcohol and a good time. She stood up and he walked toward her. "Paige, damn you look good."

He was drunk and she hated him more. She greeted him with a cold hug and he planted a kiss on her face. Along with the liquor he had the scent of perfume and pussy on his body. "I love you, Paige. I'm so fucking glad you're home. It seems like just yesterday."

"Not for me. It seems like an eternity."

"Your loyalty is amazing to me and I'm gonna prove to you that I can be that nigga in your life."

Paige nodded yes.

"Let's get dressed and celebrate! My bitch home!" He was overly excited and in her opinion doing too much.

"Let's chill for tonight, baby. I have a lot on my mind and I want to relax."

"You sure, babe? I figured since you been on lockdown for seven months that you would want to turn up and have a little fun."

"Trust me, there will be plenty time for fun. Right now all I want to do is get some more sleep and think about my future."

"With me right?" He asked with raised eyebrows.

"All of my plans for a future pertain to you, Push. Every last one of them."

CHAPTER THIRTEEN

PAIGE

"So what do you want me to do again?" The Crackhead asked Paige as they sat in a truck with tinted windows outside of Lala's house. The vehicle belonged to one of the girls that she was cool with from the strip club she used to work at and she had intentions of using it for her own devious purposes.

Although the Crackhead was on drugs she was still cute enough that her face didn't look ran into the ground. This characteristic was needed for Paige's plan to go through it.

Paige's eyes stay glued on Lala as she washed dishes in the sink of her kitchen. *What kind of stupid bitch would keep their window open when they have beef?*

The hateful glare Paige threw her was so intense it's a wonder why Lala couldn't feel the rage. "I want you to knock on the door and tell her to come outside. That you are her brother's--,"

100   By Sante' Porter

"But why?"

"Does it make a difference?" Paige yelled. "You getting money for it so what's the problem?"

She shrugged. "I don't know, it seems weird if ya'll are friends that you can't knock on the door yourself."

Paige rolled her eyes and tried to maintain her calm. "Listen, don't worry about all that. Tell her who you are and then point to this truck. I'll beep the horn and do the rest."

"That's stupid. She's gonna see right through me."

Paige leveled a sinister glare at her and said, "When are you going to realize that you not getting your next fix without this paper?" She reached in her pocket and pulled out a roll. "And you not getting shit until you do what I need done. Now go to the fucking door!"

The Crackhead looked out the window and exhaled. "I was just making a suggestion, no need to get excited."

"Well leave the suggestions to me because that ain't what I'm paying you for. Now move."

"Aight, man."

The Crackhead was about to exit the car until Paige grabbed her wrist. "I know where you live and if I feel like you're doing anything but what I told you to I'll come for you the next day and deal with you accordingly. Okay?"

The Crackhead exited the car and walked toward the house. Taking one last look at Paige before she reached the steps, she almost stumbled. When she was there she took a deep breath and knocked softly. Paige could see Lala dry her hands disappearing from the window to answer the door. Second's later, Lala opened the door.

The Crackhead said a few words to Lala and pointed at the truck. Paige sunk down in the seat and beeped the horn. Lala squinted a little and disappeared into the house, closing the door. Paige's temples throbbed as she watched the Crackhead approach the vehicle again. "What happened?"

"She said she's gonna call her brother because she don't recognize the truck."

"Fuck!"

"I did what you wanted, can I have my money now?"

"Get the fuck out of my face!" Paige yelled. "You failed and not getting shit from me."

"But I—"

When she saw the .45 sitting in Paige's lap she backed away from the window and ran down the street. *Stupid bitch.* Paige thought to herself.

She was just about to pull off when Lala came outside and moved toward the car. Paige was so scared she shook. When Lala finally approached, wearing a smile on her face Paige pointed the gun at her head. "Get...get..." The gun slipped and fumbled around but she got it together and aimed again. "Get inside." This was her first time doing anything like this but she had plans to see it through.

"Please don't do this, Paige!" Her eyes were wide. "I'm not even fucking with—"

"Get in the fucking car!" Lala slowly slid inside, closed the door and leaned up against the window. She trembled. "I have to know, what made you come out here? I know this don't look nothing like your brother's ride."

"I couldn't get a hold of him." She trembled. "So I thought she was telling the truth."

Paige shook her head. "I'm gonna ask you something and understand that I already know the answer. Are you still fucking Push?"

Tears rolled down her face. "He said he wasn't dealing with you anymore. And that ya'll broke up when you went to jail."

Paige raised the gun. "So the answer is yes?" She yelled.

"Yes, and I'm so sorry, Paige. I thought you were in jail for a long time and I—"

"Drink this shit," Paige said interrupting her. She handed her a grape soda with the top open. "Every drop."

"What is it?"

"Do you really want to refuse me? Or should I just shoot you in the face. It's your call because for real I don't give a fuck."

Lala took the drink with trembling hands. She took sip by sip until it was all gone. When she was done she wiped

By Sante' Porter

her mouth with the back of her hand. "Why are you doing this?"

"My kids have been adopted out. Because I went to jail for what I did to you." Tears rolled down Paige's cheeks. "The only thing I wanted outside of Push was my kids back and that will never happen and it's all because of your simple ass. And that dumb nigga."

"Paige, I feel like you taking this out on me for no reason. I'm a victim in this shit just like you are." Her leg shook uncontrollably as she considered fighting Paige.

"I'm sorry, do you have kids that I don't know about?"

"No, but I was pregnant when Push got with you. He left me for you and I had a late term abortion. Had to go out of the country because nobody here would do the procedure." Lala yawned. "But...but..."

Paige noticed she was getting sleepy and she relaxed a bit. "If I thought I could let you stay in this house and Push not get to you I would. But you're as weak for him as I am and you have to pay for that. I'm sorry. This is the kind of shit that can happen when you fuck with the wrong nigga."

"Please, please..." she fell into a deep sleep and Paige pulled off toward her next destination.

The lights were dim in Push and Paige's luxurious house. Plush cream carpet covered the floors and the furniture was elaborate. In the kitchen the smell of steak, potatoes, spinach and apple pie were abundant. Paige pranced around her kitchen awaiting Push's arrival. If she timed herself correctly it would be in any minute now.

"There my bitch go," Push said walking into their home.

Paige rolled her eyes out of view. "Here I am."

He walked up to her, wrapped his arms around her waist and kissed her softly on the neck. Her skin crawled despite no matter how many times she saw Push, her not being able to get over how handsome he was.

"You're making my favorite I see. What's the occasion?" He questioned rubbing his belly. "Because this look good as

By Sante' Porter

shit."

"Well we never got a chance to celebrate me being home from prison so I figured we'd start here."

"Damn, babe, you know how to do it even though I wanted to take you out." He slapped her ass. "Let me make a phone call right quick and I'll be back."

Push went into the room, made calls to his business partners and tried to reach Lala again. Normally he wouldn't try to juggle two chicks at once but something about Lala and Paige had him wanting both of them.

It was greed.

Once again he couldn't get through to her. He was just about to see what Paige was up to in the kitchen when his phone rang. "Push, this, this is..." He could barely make out what the woman was saying because her voice sounded shaken.

"Who this?"

"This is Lala's mother, she, she killed herself!"

He felt like a boulder had been dropped in the pit of his stomach. "What are you talking about? I just saw her the other day!"

"She fucking committed suicide!"

Now he understood. "But that's not like her. She would never...never..." The air seemed to be taken from his body preventing him from saying more.

"Well she did and the suicide letter she mailed to my house said it was because of you! And I hate you for it!"

CHAPTER FOURTEEN

PAIGE

Push, Paige and Orlando were watching an MMA fight over the house. They were sitting on the sofa watching the 60-inch wall-mounted flat screen TV. Orlando came over to keep Push company after learning that Lala killed herself. The worst part was not being able to tell Paige what was wrong because he should've never been in love with another woman to begin with.

"What the fuck is Liddell doing now?" Orlando asked looking at the television. "He getting his ass whopped."

Push downed some more liquor and his head rolled backwards. He was fried. "I don't even know, man." He was a hot mess.

Orlando looked at Paige and shook his head. He was so drunk now they both wondered if he even knew what was happening in the fight. She got up, walked toward the kitchen and sobbed. Orlando got up and followed her.

"Don't worry about Push, he gonna be 'aight."

She placed her hands on the counter. "But what's going on? He's not talking to me." She was acting clueless to activate the next part of her plan and Orlando was none the wiser.

"It ain't nothing harsh." He waved at the air. "Just some street shit."

"Well why is he acting like his best friend died? I never seen him like that."

Orlando exhaled, not knowing how to handle the situation. "I wish I could say more than what I've already said but I can't. That nigga would kill me if I even thought about it."

Paige, faking frustration, sighed loudly and dropped her head backwards.

When Orlando saw Paige's mood, he placed a soft hand over hers. "Just let me handle him. A few days from now he's gonna be as good as new." He paused. "But how are you doing? You know settling back home and shit. Really?"

"You mean outside of trying to find a reason to make this fucking relationship work?"

He chuckled. "You got it, gangsta. Always bringing it back to my man."

"Outside of not having my kids it's the only area in my life where I don't have control, Orlando." She threw her hands up in the air. "Why you ask anyway? I know you don't care."

"Because you look like you have a lot on your mind. Even before Push was acting fucked up."

"I'll be fine. I don't have a choice." She exhaled and grabbed one of her wine coolers from the fridge. "What I want to know is why you pretending to care when I know you don't give a fuck?"

"My bad, did I do something to you?" he pointed at his chest. "Because if I did I apologize. All I'm trying to do is make a little small talk. I can leave you alone if you want."

She exhaled. "I'm sorry. That came out fucked up, that's all."

When they heard snores they both looked into the living room and Push was out cold. "I knew he wasn't gonna be able to finish watching that fight."

"So I guess you about to leave now then. With your man sleep and all." Her voice was soft. "Right?"

"I mean I can stay, if you want me to."

"I'm just not trying to be alone right now."

He looked at his watch. "Everything I had to do was earlier. I can chill if you want."

"I want."

He looked into her eyes and looked away quickly, realizing his error. Push was snoring crazily in the other room and nobody wanted to wake him. They talked about Orlando's girlfriend, who had a toe-sucking fetish. An hour passed and they were laughing so hard you would've thought they were good friends.

And then the tone grew serious. "You know I really appreciate this right?"

He shrugged. "This not even about nothing."

"I'm for real, Orlando. You didn't have to stay but you did because I needed you to and I know none of his other friends would have."

"Why you say that?"

"Because none of them like me."

"That's a lie." She laughed and he laughed too. "Well, you right, they don't fuck with you but that's only because Push been serious since you been in the picture."

She looked at him and tilted her head. If fucking other bitches was his idea of serious all of them were crazy. "You don't have to lie, Orlando. Push and me already talked about Lala and I know he probably still fucking with her.

Orlando sat back in the chair, trying to determine if he could trust her with this tiny piece of information. He figured it wouldn't hurt for Paige to know that Lala was dead even though he was unaware that she caused her demise when she poisoned her. He was looking at the killer in the face and didn't know it.

"Paige, between me and you Lala can't be in the picture anymore because she's dead."

Paige faked surprise. "Dead?"

"Yeah…"

"Oh my God! I didn't know."

"I know, but don't say nothing about it to Push," he whispered. "Just didn't want you worrying about dumb shit."

"I won't." She said shaking her head. "And thank you. Very much, Orlando for telling me."

He shrugged. "Like I always say it ain't about nothing."

"Well your nothing is way better than a lot of other people's." She paused. "Its late, you don't need to watch me. I'm good now."

"Unfortunately I can't do that. I mean leave."

Her eyes widened. "Why?"

"Because I told you five personal stories to your one." He paused and sat back in the chair. "So you owe me."

She laughed. "Okay, so what do you want to know?"

"Something you haven't told anybody."

Her eyebrows rose. "Not even Push?"

"That's up to you."

She grinned and looked up at the ceiling. She was surprised at how easily he was falling into her hands. "I thought of something but it may be too early to tell."

"What is it? I'm ready for it."

"I think I got a crush?"

He moved around uneasily. "On who?"

"What are ya'll doing in there?" Push asked rubbing his stomach before burping. His head bobbled again.

Orlando hit the table and walked toward him, low-key mad that he didn't get Paige's answer. "We in there talking about your drunk ass since you passed out. What you doing, nigga?"

"Well who won the fight?"

Orlando looked at Paige and back at Push. "I don't know, but for real it don't even matter."

CHAPTER FIFTEEN
PAIGE

O rlando was in Push's house with Paige counting money. Normally Push left her out of his dope shit but he had an unexpected layover with his flight, after leaving town on business and wouldn't be home until tomorrow. And since the money was collected today he figured having his fiancé and best friend counting it would be okay. The thing was, the currency counter was broke which meant it had to be done by hand.

Every dollar.

"You sure you counted that right?" Paige asked him. "Because it looks like you missed a bill." Her knee brushed against his thigh accidently as they sat at the kitchen table.

"Now you got me confused." He admitted.

"Guess we gonna have to do it again." She sighed as if this wasn't all her plan.

"I'm not gonna lie, I need to rest my eyes for a minute."

He stood up and walked to the refrigerator. "Want a beer?" She nodded yes and he popped the top on two Coronas before handing her one. "So how have things been since I last talked to you?"

"Better."

"Well you don't sound too sure about that."

She laughed. "Did he love Lala more than me?"

He placed his beer on the table and turned his chair so that he could look into her eyes. "Don't put me in that kind of situation. You should be asking Push that shit."

"I just want the truth, Orlando."

"Listen, what I shared with you the night of the fight was wrong. I violated many codes by telling you that she died. Don't put me in that kind of spot again."

"It's not because I want to inconvenience you," she said. "I just want the truth and I was hoping you would understand that."

"Well why do I detect a little animosity in your voice?" He winked.

She got up, grabbed her beer and walked to the counter. "I'm going to be real with you. I don't think me and Push gonna make it. And I'm planning to tell him in a few days. And then I'm leaving him for good."

His eyes widened. "Why you gonna do that?"

"Trust. We have none."

"Then why would you burden me with some shit like that?"

"Burden you?" she frowned. "I figured you wanted to know, since the lines of communication between us were open. But I knew I should've never trusted you." She shook her head. "I'm not a good judge of character at all."

He sighed. "That's not fair."

"But it's true."

He shook his head. "What kind of nigga would I be if I gave you every step of the man's business? Huh? Would you fuck with a nigga like me?"

"Why would I fuck with you anyway? You not my man."

He swallowed. "I didn't mean it that way."

By Sante' Porter

"Then how did you mean it?" She lowered her head. "I'm so frustrated, Orlando. And all I wanted was someone to talk to about this shit." She placed the beer down on the counter. "If I leave him, where will I end up? I've been to prison for this dude and for what?"

Orlando frowned because he didn't want to hear her words although he wasn't sure why. "Then don't leave him. You sound like you've made up your mind."

"That's too easy. Don't you think?"

"We talked about it a little but how did you end up with Push?"

Mesmerized, Paige went on to give him her story, leaving nothing out. She told him about her boss who she gave oral sex to, just to keep her job, only to be fired anyway. She even told him how her kids were taken away as she went to get food in a carryout. When she was done she was mentally exhausted. It wasn't part of the plan but it was important that he trusted her more than she trusted herself. So she had to be honest about some things.

"If you feel so strongly about Push and not trusting him, why be with him?" Orlando said out of the blue. "Why live in his house and allow yourself to be emotionally abused? I'm not saying that he *is* treating you foul but if that's how you feel maybe you should leave."

"Because I'm not strong enough," she sobbed.

Orlando stood up and pulled her into his arms and allowed her to cry into his chest. He never removed his hands as she broke down. Paige spent thirty minutes spewing fake feelings and when she was done she looked up at him and their lips met.

"I shouldn't be doing this shit, Paige," he said kissing her softly again. "I can't save you."

When their lips pressed tighter together and she felt him pulling away she grabbed him harder. "I don't need saving. I just need you for one night. Can you do that for me?"

"But this is wrong."

"Why it's gotta be wrong? You need me and I need you. Have you ever thought that it could be destiny? That we came together like this? Let's just let things play out, Orlando."

After they embraced into a wide mouth kiss, which was uncommon for Paige and her rules about kissing but was an intricate part of her plan, he picked her up and gently placed her on the floor. Although Orlando was kissing her passionately, out of respect he hadn't advanced to the next level. If Paige wanted him to go all the way it would have to be her move.

Paige looked into his eyes and said, "Orlando, I want this badly, I really do."

"Are you sure?" He paused. "Because I'll be fucked up if I find out you feeling guilty when Push come home tomorrow. Only to put all of this on me."

"I know what I want, Orlando and what I want is you. That should be all the convincing you need."

To prove her point, Paige released the buttons on her blouse. When her shirt opened her red bra was exposed and her breasts spilled out.

He was rock hard.

Horny, Orlando suckled one of her nipples softly, causing electricity to shoot down to Paige's wet pussy. This was all a game to her but the experience was sure worth the risk. When he moved to the other nipple and sucked on it a little harder, milk oozed into the seat of her panties, causing her pussy to slip and slide.

Ready to fuck the brakes off of her he removed the bra completely before rubbing his hand slowly over her warm body. When the time was right, he pushed her legs open and eased his dick slowly into her hot pussy.

Paige hadn't expected Orlando to be so big and he filled her up in ways that Push never could. Orlando was a patient and considerate lover, unlike Push who needed porno sometimes to last in the bedroom. Orlando was slow and methodical with his strokes and she wanted the feeling to last forever, even if it was all a game.

He was just about to cum, when Paige looked into his eyes and boldly said; "I want you to cum in my mouth, Orlando. You gonna do that for me?"

"What?" He asked with wide eyes. He wasn't even sure if he could hold it. "You serious?" he frowned. "Because I'm not gonna treat you like no slut."

Paige was growing antsy because she wanted his mind warped when he left her. She wanted him to be thinking thoughts of her deep into his sleep. And in order to do that she had to be as freaky as possible, with the time she was allowed. "Orlando, please, I'm a big girl."

To prevent him from denying her the treat, she grabbed his dick out of her pussy, eased down and devoured it whole in her mouth. Within seconds he exploded his cum down her throat. Paige flipped her clit ferociously while his dick rested on her tongue.

Mission accomplished and yet she was just getting started.

CHAPTER SIXTEEN

PAIGE

Paige and Orlando had been sneaking around fucking for weeks. Although she enjoyed herself thoroughly she never forgot the point of her game. Everything she did held a purpose, revenge. They were in his truck behind a strip club kissing when he said; "I can't take it no more, get in the back. I gotta feel that pussy."

Paige quickly obliged. While on her knees she raised the bottom of her dress so that it draped over the top of her ass and hung at her hips. Then she placed both of her hands on the leather seat and lowered her waist until it touched the cool leather so her pussy would open up for him and as he called it, smile.

Orlando couldn't believe her sexiness and her ability to do all of the freaky things most women wouldn't. He was starting to think his friend was crazy for fucking with other bitches when he had someone who went so hard in the bedroom. Paige was first class and he loved his time with her.

With his dick rock hard, he climbed into the back seat and beat that pussy up until it was juicy, wet, and dripping everywhere. When he was finished he released all of his cum into her body as if Paige belonged to him. He was remorseless and sloppy with their fuck game.

"You gotta stop doing that," she said breathing heavily. "How we gonna explain a baby?"

"I'm sorry, you right." He rested his head on her back. "It's just that your pussy be feeling so mothafucking good."

"I bet you say that to all the girls."

"I don't," He kissed her on the back of the neck. "Because with every other girl it's not true." He sat next to her and Paige flopped down beside him, pulling her dress down. "I can't believe we still doing this."

While he pulled his pants up she looked over at him. "Orlando, just you being in the picture has given me life."

"The same here."

"I'm serious. I thought me and Push wasn't gonna work out and then here you come." She exhaled. "You came at the right time."

Orlando laughed. "Let me find out that us fucking is keeping you two together."

"Is that a problem?"

He looked ahead, out into the darkness. "I don't know what I was thinking about doing this. I never expected any of it."

She nodded. "But it's too late to wonder. We crossed boundaries a long time ago so all we can do is go with the flow."

He nodded in agreement. "And not a day goes by where I don't think this is fucked up. Like really fucked up."

She sighed. "How come you keep doing that?" She paused. "In my mind if you weren't in my life I don't know what I would do. *Seriously*. You will never know what it means to be in my position because you probably get anybody you want, in any way you want."

By Sante' Porter

"That's not true." He sighed. "I just...I just hate looking into his eyes knowing that I'm fucking his girl. It's foul on so many levels."

"Then why are you doing it?" She snapped. "If you don't want to fuck me how come you keep calling me? And asking me to meet you at this place and that place? If you want out I can give that to you, Orlando. Just say the word and stop playing games."

"Why you taking shit to the next level?"

"Because every time you cum, you try to make me feel bad because of it." She said loudly. "Like it's all my fault you fell for me."

He adjusted his body to look directly into her eyes. "Paige, calm down. I wasn't saying it that way."

"You know what, if you want me out of your life you got it."

She moved for the door and he stopped her by grabbing her wrist. "Hold up, what the fuck you doing? Leaving mad?"

"I'm not leaving mad, I'm giving you what you want, your out."

He let her go. "If you leave out of this car I will never fuck with you again. I won't call you or answer the phone if you call me."

She turned around and looked at him. "Well, I guess this is the end."

"Have I told you that I love you?" Push said, staring at Paige's reflection in the mirror as she placed on her makeup.

It took everything in her power not to throw up because love was the furthest thing from her mind. "You told me enough that I can never forget."

"Well why it sound like you don't give a fuck then?" He smiled.

She sighed. "Push, I just want to get dressed and go out with my friends."

"Where did you meet these girls from again?"

"I been knew them from the strip club."

"Well don't let them think you getting back into that lifestyle because you're not. You're about to be a married — "

When his cell phone rang, interrupting his thought, she watched him answer. He sat on the bed and said, "What up, Lando? Everything cool?"

He was silent and Paige was consumed with curiosity. "Yeah, man, that works." He paused again. "Just let me know when you gonna get it." He paused again. "Nothing, just sitting in the house." He paused again. "Yeah, Paige here, too. Why you keep asking about my girl, nigga?" He joked before pausing. "Aight, I'll get up with you later."

When he hung up he walked back over to Paige. It had been three days since she saw Orlando and he was the one who called every five minutes. At first it was to apologize about speaking to her rudely in the car and then it was to curse her out for making him fall, finally it was threats of telling Push everything. No matter what he said she didn't bite.

"Is Orlando okay?"

"I don't know what's up with that dude but I'm sick of him asking me about you every time he call. It's making me uncomfortable."

It was time to push the next part of her plan into play. "I didn't want to tell you this but you got a right to know, Orlando came on to me."

"Came on to you?" He frowned. "What the fuck you talking about?"

"It was the night you got drunk. When we were watching the fight. He even told me that you were upset about Lala being dead. Is she?"

Push's face flushed red and he moved around uneasily. "I...I don't know what he talking about."

"I could be wrong though, Push. I just wanted you to know in case he tried anything else." She kissed him on the cheek. "Let me go to the bathroom. I'll be back in the second."

She saw his face in the mirror as she walked toward the bathroom and it was stuck.

Mission accomplished.

CHAPTER SEVENTEEN

PAIGE

Orlando was extra excited as he piled into his car with Paige in his passenger seat. It had been weeks since he'd seen her, so getting a call from her in the AM gave him excitement the entire day. The anticipation of digging in that pussy drove him crazy and he was unable to focus on anything else. It helped matters that he reached out to Push on a business tip and was told he was cut off without an explanation. The only reason he didn't try proactively to get at Paige in the past was because they were friends and now that was no longer an issue since Push cut him off. If fucked him up a little but he decided to move on with Paige's head in his lap.

When they made it to a secluded motel, in Virginia, over thirty miles away from any homes or gas stations, there was an awkward feeling in the air between them. Whenever he tried to touch her she would tense up but he figured with time and a little wine she would see him the way she did in the past. But when he asked her what was wrong and she refused to answer he was more noid. However, Orlando placed so much effort into the day, he decided to give her a chance and play it easy.

After sitting on the bed she watched as Orlando unloaded wine from a paper bag that he carried. But when she pulled hers out of the bag he decided to drink hers instead after she claimed it was a favorite. He poured a glass for himself and then Paige.

"To us," he said as he raised his glass in an effort to make a toast.

"To us." She softly clinked her glass against his and said, "I missed you. A whole lot."

He took a big gulp and then another while she hadn't bothered to touch hers. "You know I'm feeling you right?" he said eyeing her closely. "And I don't care who knows it this time."

She sat her glass on the table beside the bed. "I know, Orlando. Because I feel the same way. Always have but was waiting on you to come around."

"Did you think 'bout me?" He paused before drinking the rest of his wine. "While we weren't together?"

What's up with this soft shit? She thought.

"I think about you every day but I was tired of you throwing Push in my face. If we were fucking we were fucking and that was our business. It's not like we ain't grown."

"You right." He nodded and sat next to her.

"I want to tell you something but I don't know if I can trust you."

He frowned. "Paige, I want you to know you can trust me. And I'm willing to do anything I can to prove it to you. That's on everything I hold close."

She laughed. "The funny thing is at first I was feeling like it might not work with Push. As far as our relationship and stuff. And I thought he would give me a hard time if I left him so I thought of another way out."

"What was that?"

Paige reached into her purse and pulled out a gun. Orlando jumped back until he saw how tiny and cute it was. It was a .22 and way smaller than the weapons he handled personally. He removed it from her hand and gazed at it. "Sexy, what the fuck were you gonna do with this?"

"As much damage as I could."

He laughed. "Well you'd definitely pinch him that's for sure."

"That's not funny," she pouted snatching the weapon at the barrel before dropping it back in her purse.

He scooted closer. "You know I'm just fucking with you. But you don't have to go that far, baby girl. If you want out Push gonna let you go. No need for the hardware."

"I wish I can believe you."

"You can. Me and Push got our problems but I'd hate to see him go out like that."

Can't believe this nigga still taking up for him even after being cut off. She thought.

"Anyway, I just hope you're serious about us, Orlando. No more playing games."

"I'm here because I'm really willing to give us a chance. I don't know how much more serious I can be."

"Good, I'm glad you feel that way, because I want to talk to you about some things."

"What now?" he frowned.

"You should've told me the truth about Lala when I asked. If there was any hope for you, for us even being friends, you should've kept it one hundred." She dug in her purse but his eyes remained on hers.

He chuckled, stood up and poured some more wine. "Now who's bringing up the past?"

"I'm just telling you how I feel, Orlando. You're free to roam the country if you're not interested in hearing me. I'm not stopping you."

"Why does this even matter? I'm in your life now and I don't feel comfortable with you bringing up one of Push's bitches who's not even alive. I put everything on the line to get to know you."

"And I didn't ask you to."

"I know, Paige." He sighed, frustrated already. "I know you didn't but I still did. And the only thing I want to do now is be with you. Can you understand that? Because if you can't maybe you should leave right now and trust me, this time I will never hit you again. I'm tired of this shit too."

She laughed. "It doesn't even matter." She hit the bed. "Come sit next to me."

Thinking he was about to get some pussy he sat closely to her. Before doing anything he looked at the wine glass behind her. "Before we have sex, I need you to drink that."

Her eyebrows rose. She realized he wasn't as gullible as she thought. "Wait, you think I poisoned it or something?"

In the sternest voice he ever used with her he said, "Drink...the...fucking...wine."

Paige grabbed the glass and drank it all, staring into his eyes the entire time. Then she extended her glass toward him even though it would've been too late. "Pour me another?"

He laughed, low key relieved that she didn't poison him. "Naw, I can't do that."

"Why not?"

"Because I drank it all."

"Well maybe you can do this." She reached into her purse, held the gun under his chin and pulled the trigger.

Although Orlando thought the gun was a joke she knew from research the fragments in a .22 caliber bullet could do far more damage to organs because it was harder to get tiny shrapnel out without injuring the victim even more. He also didn't notice that she slid on a glove so her fingerprints wouldn't be present. All of her tracks were covered and she loved how easily her plan had come together. Push made her a killer and she was realizing she was good at it.

Without remorse, when she was done with him she stood up, dug into his pocket and removed his cell phone. Then she sent a message to Push from it.

I thought u was a real 1. Guess not. If u lookin for me U can find me @ Chiloe. Room 134. I'm done wit it all.

By Sante' Porter

CHAPTER EIGHTEEN

PUSH

Push was in bed thinking about losing one of his closest comrades. Having to suffer with two people in his life dying from suicide seemed unreasonable but it was reality. The worst part was that Paige was nowhere to be found. Lately he was starting to realize that although he was trying to do better by her, and their relationship, Paige seemed absent and uninterested.

Sometimes she stayed out all night and when he would ask where she'd been she'd roll her eyes and remind him that she was grown. He was lost and starting to feel hate brewing up in his heart for his young fiancé.

Suddenly his body felt weaker. At first he thought he was cold until he checked his temperature and realized his body was overheating. He was about to go make some soup, when Paige strolled into the bedroom wearing a smile on her face.

She was carrying her Fendi purse and flung it on the chair in the room. "What's wrong?" She asked.

Push didn't respond, instead he remained in bed and placed his arms behind his head as he looked up at the ceiling. "Nothing."

"Push, are we really playing this game?" She sat on the edge of the bed, and rubbed his sweaty legs. "Wait, you don't feel good." Her eyebrows rose.

"I'm sick, Paige," He rolled his eyes. "A fever I think."

She flipped her hand over and felt the heat from his body via his forehead. Her eyes widened. "Oh my, God, Push, you have a fucking fever! When this happen?"

He shrugged. "I don't know. Was laying in bed and the next thing I knew I was too weak to move. I'll be alright though." He was trying to feel tough but just like most men he was a mess when sick.

"Don't worry because I'm here now and I'm gonna get you better," she said. She removed her jacket and walked into the bathroom, returning with a thermometer. "Open your mouth," she said.

He did.

"Push, we gotta bring that temperature down. Damn, I didn't know you were in here sick, why didn't you call?"

"Been hitting you all day and you still—"

"I know but you didn't say anything about you being sick," she interrupted. "I wouldn't have had you in here by yourself."

He looked into her eyes and saw she was acting differently. Something didn't feel right. "I guess I didn't think you gave a fuck."

"Push, we might have our problems but if I would've known you was like this I would've come home earlier. I'm your fiancé!" She kissed him on the head. "Now let me see if I can get you back together."

Paige rushed into the bathroom and filled the tub up with cool water knowing he probably wouldn't like it. When it was full she poured alcohol inside. When she was done she walked into the bedroom and helped Push inside the bathroom. When he was there she removed his clothing and helped him into the water.

"Paige, this shit too cold," he shivered as she cupped pockets of water with her hand and poured it all over his body.

"I know, but this the only way to lower that temperature so you gotta man up and take it." She looked into his eyes, deeply and Push could feel the love she had for him, at least he hoped so. In that moment it seemed like there was nothing more important than making him well.

Carefully and gently she continued to wipe him down with chilled water and when she was done, Paige dressed him in a pair of soft grey pajama pants and a white cotton t-shirt. Then she changed the bed with fresh sheets before helping him into the bed so that he would be comfortable.

When he was situated she brought him fresh soup and fed him. The entire time he thought about what he put her through and felt grateful even though he didn't deserve her. When he was fed he held her hand already feeling slightly better. "Paige, I want us to be right okay? I want us to start over."

"I told you it's done, Push. We together."

By Sante' Porter

"Seriously, babe. I can tell by your actions that you don't trust me and after losing Orlando I can honestly say I never want to feel like this again."

She frowned. "So it took losing Orlando for you to realize what you had in me?"

"You know what I mean."

She exhaled. "You know what, I don't want to fight with you anymore. All I want to do is hold you until you get better." She climbed into the bed, removed her shirt and pressed her breast against his back. "How does it feel?"

"It feels good."

"Feels good to me too." She kissed his back.

"Do you know that the first day I saw you, I knew you would be my wife," Push whispered. "I didn't even go that way on the regular but something told me to turn my steering wheel and there you were. Waiting for me."

She laughed. "Your ass was persistent too."

"You go after what you want in life."

She nodded. "True about that."

"We've been through a lot. More than I wanted to put you through."

"Maybe this is better, Push. Maybe you're going through this so you can understand you have to treat the people in your life right. Maybe this is all to give you a taste of your own medicine."

Push turned around and looked at her. "What you talking about? My friend killing himself is my fault?"

"Everything."

Push felt she was going too far but arguing was the last thing he wanted to do. "I don't know if that's true or not. But I do know that I've never been with anybody on this level. And I know things aren't going the way you want them to with me but they'll get better. You just gotta give a nigga some time."

"I believe you, Push." She touched his face and he was cooler than he was when she first came home. "You know what, for some reason seeing you like this got my pussy all kinds of wet."

Push felt his dick hardening and realized he was aroused too. "If I had the energy to fuck you I would." He laughed.

She sat up in the bed. "You might not have the energy to fuck me but I have the energy to suck that dick." She crouched down and gave him an epic blowjob that put him to sleep for the rest of the day.

CHAPTER NINETEEN

PAIGE

Paige sat in the living room on the sofa in her aunt Laverne's two-bedroom apartment. Laverne had been trying to reach Paige for the longest and Paige would promise to come over, only to stand her up. This time she said it was imperative and it involved her health so after nursing Push as if she really gave a fuck about him, she decided to visit Laverne.

Laverne walked up to Paige and sat next to her. "I can't believe your ass finally came over here. Do you know how long I been trying to get in contact with you?"

"Auntie, stop playing." She sighed.

She smiled. "Seriously, what made you come over?"

She laughed. "Because you said you were sick. So what's wrong?"

Laverne waived her hand. "Child, ain't nothing wrong with me. Just reached deep in the bag to get you to visit."

By Sante' Porter

Paige shook her head. "I knew that shit."

"You're not totally off the hook yet because I know you been acting out of character. And if your mother were alive she'd be disappointed. She probably rolling over in her grave."

"You don't know what you talking about," she said sitting deeper into the sofa.

"I know enough to realize that being mad at other people won't bring your boys back, Paige." Laverne looked across the living room. "So I want to know right now, do you really miss your kids?"

Paige felt her blood boiling over because she killed two people to get at the one man she felt was responsible for her not being with her children. Had it not been for fighting Lala the government would not have taken her children away permanently? Of course she loved those boys. "I'm not gonna answer that, auntie."

"I want to do something for you. Something I want to make sure you deserve."

Paige rolled her eyes. "You don't have to do anything for me."

"Except get the hate out of your heart."

Paige shook her head. "Who have you been talking to? Because you sure act like you know everything about me without talking to me."

"I spoke to Push." She paused. "Well I spoke to Push before he stopped calling months ago."

"Push? Why would you do that?"

She sighed and sat closer. "Because the lifestyle you're leading will soon end in death, Paige. And before he stopped calling he said you looked and acted differently. And now that you're in my presence I see what he's talking about. You've definitely changed...more bitter."

Paige got up to leave. "I'm gone."

"If you do, you won't see what I have for you in my room."

"What do you have? More insults?"

"How about your children?"

By Sante' Porter

Paige felt like the room was spinning. "Don't play with me, auntie. If you play with me like that I may never speak to you again. Even might fight you if I tried hard enough."

She laughed. "Your children are in the room sleep."

Paige placed her hand over her heart. "How? I...I don't understand."

"The adopted family the boys are with is the best, Paige. The best. Your children wanted to see you but instead of reaching out to you with all the drama you've been in, the social worker called me. Made me promise that I wouldn't call you."

Tears had begun to roll down Paige's face and she felt as if she were about to hyperventilate. "But why you when the boys wanted me?"

"Because the family feels its better to see a family member instead of no family member at all. Now, I know we not all that close but them boys know me like they know you."

Paige touched her chest. "Can I...can I go back...?" She pointed at her room.

Laverne smiled. "Yes, go ahead."

Paige rushed toward the room and opened the door. She pushed it open so wide it banged into the wall, imprinting a doorknob hole in the paint. Her children jumped up, rubbed their eyes and hugged her tightly. She was sobbing so much that she could barely see them.

For fifteen minutes they wept and she was amazed at how handsome and tall they were. They talked about their new school and Marcus claimed to have a girlfriend already. Laverne came inside several times as the hours passed but only to bring them food and drink. Time flew by and just being in their presence made Paige feel lighter and suddenly fighting with Push felt dumb. Maybe she was too hard on him and would rethink what she'd done. Especially since Laverne had access to the twins every month. Up until this point she thought she'd never see them again.

They were just about to watch a movie when she heard Laverne yelling and cursing at someone. Before she could find out what was happening the door flung open and a white woman she didn't know with fiery red hair was

By Sante' Porter

staring down at her. She quickly grabbed the kids by the hands and yelled, "You are not supposed to be here! This visit was approved with the aunt only."

Paige was about to hit her in the face until Laverne pulled her back. "Don't do it, Paige. Don't do it." When she felt Paige was going to hit her anyway she said, "Look at your boys. You don't want them to remember you like this."

She blinked a few times and looked down at the twins and they both looked scared. When she heard a walkie-talkie and looked into the living room and saw a police officer. She exhaled and focused on her sons. "I'm sorry...some kind of way, I will come back for you." She then focused on her aunt. "You hurt me more by giving me hope and then stealing it away. This shit has done more damage than you could ever imagine."

CHAPTER TWENTY

PAIGE

Paige's hips swerved slowly while her breasts, without a bra, bounced up and down as she danced inside Partition Club. She looked thirsty but she didn't care. Sweat glistened over her skin and the black jeans she wore squeezed her curves. But the biggest thing was that she was drunk.

Paige had the attention of every nigga in the club but she wasn't searching. She was trying to get her mind off of losing her kids again and her life, and dancing always helped. She ignored Push's calls so many times that her battery was dead.

She was just about to get in her car and go to another club when a dude name Quanta walked up to her. He was a well-known drug dealer from Baltimore who hadn't planned on staying long until he spotted Paige. Stepping up he put his hands on her waist. "What's your name, ma, because I

By Sante' Porter

know you not here by yourself?" His voice was heavy and his lips were inches away from her cheek. "Something as fine as you has to be taken so I'm here to scoop you up."

"I...I ain't...." She was so drunk her voice slurred.

His warm breath tickled her ear. "Oh hold up, you that drunk?"

"I had a little bit."

He laughed and looked down at her breasts. "You want to take a seat with me in VIP and talk about it?" He gripped her closely so that her ass was in the seat of his jeans. "Because I don't want you on the floor hurting yourself."

"I don't see why not." She wiggled her ass harder until she felt him growing.

He walked her over to VIP and she flopped onto his lap. She was playing herself like a whore. "Damn, you nice and warm." He paused. "Tell me what you doing in here by yourself?"

"Just having some fun." When a picture of the twin's faces flashed in her mind she shook her head to erase her thoughts. "If you want to be nice to me I need a drink. Two of them." She threw up the peace sign.

"You sure you can handle it?"

"Two shots of vodka."

He flagged a bartender down who filled her order. "So...you live around here?"

"I live nowhere."

While they sat on the sofa Quanta couldn't help but notice other niggas were still breaking their necks to get a good look at the loose chick. Her beauty was crucial but her sex appeal roared.

"So where you headed tonight? Because you look like you still up for some fun."

"I don't want to make plans, just wanna...wanna..." When her speech fell off she downed the two shots and wiped her mouth with the back of her hand. "Go with the flow."

"You feeling good ain't you?" Quanta said. "Want to get out of here?"

"And do what?"

"That's up to you, love. No pressure with me either which way." He paused. "By the way, what's your name?"

"Paige. But if you do me right you can call me whore."

He raised his eyebrows because she was extra loose. He felt like he hit the jackpot. "So let's leave."

"Let's go." She stood up and when she saw someone pointing at her across the way at the bar she felt her stomach flop. It was the Crackhead she had help her lure Lala to her death. "We need to leave now." Suddenly her drink was wearing off.

"Hold up, ma. What's wrong?"

She grabbed his hand but he remained planted. When he saw the Crackhead talking to a dude he released her hand. "I was up for some pussy but I'm not about to fight over you either." He pushed her away. "I'm out."

The moment he was gone the Crackhead was in front of her, blocking her path. "You killed that girl!" She yelled pointing in her face. "Didn't you?"

"I don't know what you talking about!"

She tried to move again but the Crackhead grabbed her hair. Had she not been so drunk she could've defended herself. "You killed her and you made me help you!"

She was yelling so loudly that other people were starting to look in their direction. Paige new she had to do something or people would start listening and may tell the cops about a murder that was ruled a suicide. So using all of her drunken strength, she hit the Crackhead in the mouth. But she was so drunk there wasn't much force.

In the end the Crackhead beat her so badly that a fine cutie separated from his friends to help her out. He had been looking at her all night but Quanta laid plans making her inaccessible. He would've rather her be in good health but he would take her as he could get her.

The first thing he did was pull the Crackhead off of Paige. When she tried to jump he said, "I'm a dude, don't make me drop you."

The Crackhead, already out of breath decided not to challenge him. "You better be careful, she's trouble." She stomped away.

By Sante' Porter

When she was gone he checked on Paige. "You good?"

"Yeah," she said huffing harshly. "But I want to get out of here."

"Okay let me make the introductions quick. My name's Vincent, what's yours?"

"Paige..." She touched her lips because she could feel they were swollen.

"So where are your friends, Paige? Because I know you didn't come out here alone."

"I don't have any friends and you could say I am solo."

He nodded. "Well you want me to call your man to come get you?"

"I don't have one of those either."

He nodded. "Well my car is out front. If you want you can roll with me."

"Can I get you guys something else to drink?" a bartender asked approaching the duo. His eyes were fixated onto Paige who was just beaten within every inch of her life.

"We good." Vincent said. "But thanks, man."

"Okay…let me know if you need me." He picked up a few glasses that had fallen over in VIP after the fight.

"So what's the move?"

She sighed and realized she wasn't prepared to be with Push either. She held him personally responsible for her troubles and she would never get over it. "I guess I'm coming with you."

He grinned. "Let's bounce."

CHAPTER TWENTY-ONE

PAIGE

Paige and Vincent were sitting on the sofa inside of a mid-level hotel. He stopped by the liquor store at her request and his only hope was that she wouldn't be too drunk to fuck. Although he appreciated her looseness, he didn't like his women corpse-like either.

"So you gonna stop playing games and get revenge on that nigga you mad at? Because I know that's the reason you're here."

Her eyes fluttered and her head, which was extremely heavy, rolled. How did he know? "I don't know about all that."

He laughed. "I know a woman who's been hurt when I see one." He paused. "So why you making things hard, Miss Paige? Let's do what we came to do."

"I'm not trying to make things hard for you, Vincent." Wobbling a little, she stood in front of him and dropped her jeans. "I was just giving you a chance to...to warm up."

He smiled. "I been warm since the moment I saw you."

He grabbed her drink and sat it on the floor. "All I want to do is make you smile."

"Prove it," he said, trying to ignore her sex appeal by appearing unbothered. It was mission impossible, considering his dick was rising like fresh dough inside his jeans.

She dropped down, wiggled between his thighs and placed her hands on his knees. She looked up at him and noticed he seemed surprised. Her plan was to be as nasty as possible with a complete stranger. She wanted to slut herself out, out of guilt for being a bad mother, losing her kids, killing Lala and even Orlando. She wondered repeatedly since she murdered him if it wasn't a mistake. And this was her way of giving herself punishment, knowing the risks were plenty.

"Are you serious?" he asked excitedly. "You gonna top me off?"

"Dead ass," she said shaking her head slowly from left to right.

"You don't know how much you looking out I had a rough day."

"I'm glad I can do this for you." She lowered the zipper on his jeans and unleashed his dick.

He swallowed the lump in his throat when he felt the cold air rushing against his stick. She kissed the tip of his dick and ran her tongue around the hole like she did with Push when things were good between them.

"Damn, girl. Why you doing that shit so—"

Before he could finish his statement his dick was between her plush lips. He would be lying if he said he thought he would receive such a treat. Paige looked more like a good girl on the verge of bad behavior but he was glad he was wrong.

When his legs wouldn't open wide enough she pushed his jeans toward his ankles. "I like it better this way."

When his naked ass was on the sofa, Paige gripped his stick, pursed her lips and blew soft blasts of air onto the tip.

He stiffened harder when her slimy tongue slithered up and down his balls. Just when he thought she'd done enough she sucked on his nut sack like a cherry.

"You taste as sweet as I imagined," she complimented.

Vincent closed his eyes and let her do her thing. Seconds later he felt her feather soft hairbrush against his thighs. Paige licked him for as long as she could without allowing him to bust a nut.

"I know you didn't bring me here to get topped off. I want to get right too." She stood before him, pussy dripping wet waiting for him to take her.

Vincent removed a condom and slid it on his stick. Paige quickly rose, eased out of the rest of her clothes and lowered her body. His dick parted her strawberry-pink pussy lips as he pushed deeper into her tunnel. When she heated up Vincent gripped her waist and fucked her like she owed him money.

"Damn you feel good, Paige," He said. "Pussy tight too."

"Don't say my name, baby," she suggested. "Call me a bitch."

His eyes widened. "For real?"

"Are you gonna fuck this up for me or do what I asked?" She questioned.

He shrugged and gave her what she wanted, while adding a few lines too. "Keep it right there, stupid bitch! Just like that!"

He called her everything but her first name and it felt so good that at some points she wanted to cry and at other times she wanted to cum. Suddenly the guilt she felt earlier was wearing off. Maybe it was her fault the twins were taken and maybe she should give Push another chance, especially since she was getting revenge dick.

"Keep it like that, nigga," she said wiggling her hips.

When it got too good to him Vincent lifted her and bent her body over the arm of the sofa. The juice from her wet pussy drizzled from his dick and slapped against the carpet. Spreading her legs wider, he rammed his thickness as deep as it would go. When he felt his cum drawing nearer, he pawed at her breasts and used them as reigns to go harder from behind.

He was in heaven until he realized it was feeling too good. Instead of stopping he continued to pound on her until his semen splashed into her body, already knowing the condom had broken. Luckily she came too and when she did he yanked his dick out and grabbed the shredded condom before she saw it.

Exhausted both of them flopped to the couch. "I guess we didn't need the bed huh?"

She shrugged. "I guess not."

"Feel better now?"

She laughed. "I do."

He stood up and grabbed his jeans. "Well you can leave when you want the room's paid up for the night. I'm going back to the club to pick up my friends."

She could care less. "I understand."

After he cleaned himself up he noticed she was sleep on the sofa, ass naked, as she was when he left her. Since he thought she was on the verge of going to the wild side

By Sante' Porter

unless he slowed her down he decided to leave her a note before he left. When he was done he walked out the door.

Paige had five hours of sleep when her cell phone rang. She didn't even remember charging it up in Vincent's car on the way to the hotel. Head pounding due to the sun pouring inside of the room, she grabbed her cell off the table. "Paige, why you haven't been answering my calls?" Push sounded frantically. "And where you at?" he sounded alarmed.

She swallowed the dry taste from her mouth. "I'm sorry…I wanted to…I wanted to be alone."

"Babe, we gotta stop doing this shit to each other. Meet me later so we can talk. With all the stuff going on now I need you and I want to work on our family. Okay?"

She nodded. "Okay, Push. I'll see you in a little while." She ended the call and looked down at the note on the table. Her heart almost stopped and it confirmed that she needed to slow down.

It read:

You seem cool so let me give you this gift. Don't pick up niggas from the club. The condom broke and it's fucked up because I go both ways. I suggest you get tested. I haven't been in years.

By Sante' Porter

CHAPTER TWENTY-TWO
PAIGE AND PUSH

Paige and Push sat in an elegant restaurant within the Gaylord at the National Harbor. The all black suit he sported showed off his handsome features while Paige was equally beautiful with the black dress she wore which exposed just enough cleavage to cause other male customers to gaze her way constantly.

"Paige," he said placing his hand over hers. "What's on your mind? And I want you to be real with me."

She exhaled. "I want to talk to you about how I've been feeling but I don't know if I can trust you. Or if you'll be real with me."

He removed his hand and wiped his mouth with the napkin. "Just tell me." He cleared his throat, fearing the worst. "Let's start there because I want to get shit out in the open and it's obvious things aren't right between us."

"I'm worried that you'll cheat on me again. And I can't

take it."

He leaned in. "Cheat?"

"Don't act like you haven't in the past."

He sat back and sighed.

Hearing the words *cheat* was the furthest thing from his mind but at least he knew what was troubling her. "What can I do to let you know I'm different now? Where can we go from here?" He paused. "Because over the past few weeks you've been acting like you don't fuck with me. And as much as I love you, I'm not gonna tolerate you staying out overnight. Ever again. Not if you want to be with me."

She sat back in the seat and puffed. "Push, I've done some things, some things I'm not proud of."

His eyebrows rose. "Like cheating?"

"Don't turn this around on me," she said. As if she wasn't worried sick about what Vincent told her last week at the hotel. Although she went to the doctor and had a clean bill of health she knew she had to check herself regularly to be sure. "I'm not the one stepping out sexually in this relationship."

By Sante' Porter

"Then what you mean?"

"I mean I've been feeling a lot of evil things toward you and I'm tired of being heavy." She paused. "I want this to work but not if the games are gonna persist. You'd do better just to let me go."

"What do you want me to do? Turn back time?"

"Don't be stupid." She paused. "But what do you want *me* to do? Forget you ever cheated?"

He sighed. "I failed you, Paige. And all I can say is I'm sorry." He touched her hand. "But tell me if I'm fighting this battle alone because I'm trying to marry you tomorrow."

Her eyes widened. "Tomorrow?"

He grinned. "Yes, I mean aren't you ready?"

She looked around, confused. She hadn't expected him to move so quickly. "I'm trying to figure that out."

He slammed his napkin down and shook his head. He was trying to be sensitive to her feelings but the melodrama level was high. After all, it wasn't like he dogged her out as badly as he'd done some of the other chicks. Lala lost her life fucking with him so he thought.

"Give me one month, Paige. Just one month. If you decide you not fucking with me again I'll leave you alone. I'll let you go with no strings." He poured his heart out and the only thing Paige did was roll her eyes. "What you going to do?"

She sat back and looked over at him. "Push, I need time. And if you knew the things I was capable of you would back off and give it to me."

"But I'm ready for you to be my wife."

"Why? So if you cheat again I won't leave you? Because that paper don't mean shit to me. If I'm hurt again I can be dangerous."

He didn't believe her and instead thought she was precious. "I know you will never hurt me," he said arrogantly. "You love me so much."

"Don't be so sure."

He chuckled softly, done fighting with her. "Let's get out of here, so you can take that anger out on me in the bedroom. I wanna hear you talk that shit then."

Crouched over Push, Paige lowered her head over his dick. Push was so aroused at her extra freakiness that he oozed pre-cum. Push moaned louder than he ever had as her tongue circled and traced the base of his pole.

The girl sure did love sucking dick.

He palmed her head and fucked her mouth. Paige was a trooper and didn't gag once. And he rewarded her buy shooting a trail of cream down her throat. But she hadn't gotten hers yet so she crawled on top of him, dripping wet and all.

"Wake that dick up, nigga," She demanded. "We just getting started."

Knowing he liked when she talked shit he stiffened inside of her and he gripped her hips as he felt himself ready to go the extra mile. The more she talked the harder he came and he realized there was no turning back for them. They were in this relationship until death do they part.

She came hard and he came again afterwards she collapsed on his chest. "You trying to kill me?"

"Naw, just want to love you." She ran her finger through the grooves of his chest.

"Well you stay right there." He slapped her ass. "I'm gonna drain the weasel and I'll be right back."

When he ran to the bathroom she figured she would take a nap until she felt something vibrating under her head. Curious, she lifted the pillow and couldn't find the phone but she knew it was ringing. When she realized the pillow was heavier than usual she stuck her hand inside of it and frowned when she saw his makeshift-hiding place.

Push had cut a slit within his personal pillow, making a pocket for his cell phone. But she caught his ass anyway. When she removed it and looked at the text message her stomach swirled.

WYD? Its messed up I haven't heard from U since we hooked up. Niggas told me not 2 mess with u. I shoulda listened.

Paige's skin was red hot. She didn't understand why he thought she was a game. It was obvious that once a cheat

By Sante' Porter

always a cheat. As she lie on her back she looked at the beautiful home she was living in. She liked her lifestyle and didn't want it to change.

She had to think straight.

She had to be smart.

But she had to attack.

CHAPTER TWENTY-THREE
PUSH AND PAIGE

Push's house was bustling with people who attended the wedding. Push and Paige were officially husband and wife. It was a small-scale ceremony because Paige didn't want anything major and he decided to hold the reception at his house per her wishes. It was like she was trying to keep their union a secret, something that shocked him since women always wanted to be his wife.

In the dining room, away from the crowd sat Push, Paige and Mick. She could tell Mick didn't like her but she could care less. She had the man and her plans would go down unhinged.

Paige, who hadn't said one word to Mick rubbed Push's shoulders. "Can I get you anything, husband?" She kissed his cheek. "Damn...you're my husband. I love it."

He smiled, realizing he liked the sound of her words. "Naw, babe. I'm gonna kick it with Mick for a minute and meet you out there with the rest of the guests." It was obvious his man had something to say to him and he wanted to give him the honor of doing it in private.

"Well don't be too long," she said before rolling her eyes at Mick. "Your wife wants a little alone time."

"I just need five minutes."

Paige stood up and walked toward the kitchen leaving the men alone.

When she was gone Mick said, "I know this the wrong time, since you married her and all, but I think you made a mistake."

Push laughed. "And you telling me this now?"

"I know it's crazy but I would kill myself if I didn't say anything ever."

"Don't play like that, slim". Push said seriously looking into Mick's eyes silently making reference to the fact that he's lost one too many people by suicide already. "It's not funny."

Mick realized his slip up. "My bad, bruh. I just really got a lot on my head about Paige."

"I'm not leaving my wife, Mick so you can leave it alone," Push responded coldly.

"I understand that but I'm afraid if I don't say something now things will get worse. Like it did with Lala and Lando."

Push wiped his eyes and looked over at him. "What you saying? My wife was responsible for that shit?"

"I'm saying I don't trust your wife." He said sternly. "I have a feeling she was fucking Orlando, got him strung out and killed the nigga to get at you. She's slick, man. And I know you can feel it."

Push's nostrils flared. "I know that's not true. I know you not telling me now that my wife fucked my friend after he's dead and gone."

"I thought you told me Paige said he came on to her. A few days before he died."

"Yeah, but she also said she had him wrong."

"So why did you end the friendship? Because Orlando was fucked up by that."

"You making huge accusations now, Mick. And what went on between me and Lando was our business. Tread easily."

"I know I am which is why I don't take what I'm saying lightly." He paused. "Since she's been in the picture everybody dead but me. And I refuse to go anywhere. And if something happens to you she better hope I never find her."

"Even if I wanted to believe this shit, how you figure she was involved?" Push frowned.

"I walked up to Orlando on some business shit one day and he was on the cell phone. I think it was with her because I saw Paige on his screen and he looked stuck when I caught him. He hung up without even saying bye. Later on that day you found him dead in the motel room. It don't get much creepier than that."

"What was said?" Push continued.

"Something about he couldn't wait to see her." He paused. "I got the impression he was meeting with whoever was on that phone."

Push leaned back because he couldn't imagine his meek wife being so hostile. Yeah she threatened him in the beginning. But she never hit him or acted out violently in any way. "So basically you have no facts, just accusations." Push said through squinted eyes.

"I'm serious, man."

"Is that why you're telling me this shit right now, Mick? I mean what you want me to do even if it is true? Divorce her?"

Mick ran his hand down his face. "I don't know what I want you to do, man. And I know it sounds bad." He paused. "This is why it took me so long to come to you with this shit. But I can't hold back no more. Your wife don't seem right. I even seen her a few times hanging in the doorway when we talking business. I looked at her when I noticed and she ran off. She's keeping tabs on you. I think she's keeping tabs on me too."

Push's temples throbbed and he stroked them. "She's my wife, man. You hear me? My wife. If you want that to change you have to give me more because nothing I hear makes me wanna bounce."

"It still don't change the fact that maybe she's not the one."

Push stood up. "I'm not listening to this shit no more." He paused. "Get the fuck up out my house."

"What?" Mick frowned.

"I'm not about to let you stand up in my house and disrespect her. If you don't like her don't come around."

"Fuck is you saying really, Push?" Mick yelled. "That girl got you so fucked up you can't see your friend is spitting real shit?"

"What I see is that today I married the love of my life. And instead of you being happy for me, you shitting on the entire day. And I can't have that."

"You taking this thing to another level now," Mick said. "I'm not the enemy. You married her."

"Why don't you do me a favor and bounce," Push said pointing toward the front of the house.

"Are you sure about this shit?"

"Did I stutter?"

When Mick left, Paige walked back into the dining room holding a glass of Hennessey for him. "What was that all about?" She frowned. "Mick ran out slamming the door?"

"How 'bout you tell me," Push said sharply. The seeds of her betrayal were planted in his mind and it caused him to question their bond. "Let's start there."

"Wait, he gets mad at you and now you mad at me?" Paige sat in a chair next to him ready to do collateral damage. "What's going on, Push? We just got married. Don't let somebody fuck that up."

"Are you doing right by me? Can I really trust you?"

With a smile she said, "Push, you know that—"

"I need you to answer the fucking question straight up, Paige! Can I trust you or not?"

His raised voice frightened her. "I just vowed my life to you, in front of a lot of people. Of course you can trust me."

"Then why is Mick making me feel that you may have fucked Orlando behind my back? I mean did you?"

Paige moved uneasily in her seat. "I told you all I know about Orlando. We never had a relationship. You have to remember, I'm the one who came to you about him in the first place. Right? Why would I do that and then cheat? It doesn't make any sense." She touched his hand. "We're married and you belong to me now. Remember? I own you."

CHAPTER TWENTY-FOUR

PAIGE

Paige sat in her aunt's house and ate a homemade pizza, using a recipe Laverne use to make when Paige was a kid. It was a favorite then and a favorite at the moment. When the meal was over she sat back and rubbed her stomach. "Thanks, auntie."

"A thank you is nice but I would've preferred an invitation to your wedding."

Paige sighed and rolled her eyes. "It wasn't that big of a deal, trust me."

"How it's not a big deal for you to get married?"

She smiled. "Everything is not what it seems."

She nodded. "So how have you been getting on? Since the last time you saw the twins?"

"You're playing right?" She frowned. "Because if you're not I'm going to need you to not ask me anything so stupid again."

By Sante' Porter

"Well I can tell that you're still angry." She continued. "And I can't say that I don't understand, because I do, now I'm afraid about something you said to the social worker."

"That night is all a blur but I'm sure you remember don't you, auntie," Paige said sharply. "I don't know what the problem is anyway. Besides, I have a right to be angry at a man who was the cause of my kids being taken away from me."

"Paige, that ship has sailed. The only thing you can do now is plan how you will be a good wife, and a better woman. You can always have more kids. Your life is not over."

Paige's head rotated swiftly in her direction. "Last week, after the wedding, I had my tubes tied. If I can't have the twins I will never be a mother again."

Laverne was devastated. "Oh, Paige. Why would you do something so permanent?"

"Because I don't want to be in that kind of pain anymore. Ever. And unless you've had kids, which you haven't, you can't understand what that feels like." Paige seemed heavy just thinking about her loss again. "You never cared about me did you? You wanted nothing to do with me before my mother asked you to come get me on her deathbed." Paige was beyond angry and wild thoughts circulated in her mind. And then she scratched her head. "But that's ancient history, fuck that what I want to know is this, how come you couldn't get the twins? When I asked, cause I know you love them."

"Paige, don't do that."

"I want to know! Right now they're living with some people who will never allow me to have anything to do with them. You could've saved me but you didn't."

Laverne sighed. "I wasn't going to tell you this but you might as well know now. I'm sick, Paige. Have been for a few years."

"But you said you weren't! When I came over that day."

"I know but the boys were here and I wanted that moment for you. Sometimes I have good days but lately they have been bad. The last thing I wanted was to bring those kids here only to die on them."

By Sante' Porter

Paige's eyes widened with concerned but then the emotion quickly evaporated. "I could've helped you with them. Then me and my children would've stayed together."

"That may be true some but I can't take it back now."

"You abandoned me when I needed you and I hate you for it."

Laverne sighed and sat closer to her. "I was in no position to be to those kids what they needed and it's obvious you weren't either or else they would not have taken them. Now if you need someone to hate at night to make you sleep easier than so be it. But let me clear something up, blame doesn't make the pain go away."

"You know what, fuck you!"

Laverne slapped her so hard it took almost a minute for the sting to go away. "You don't have a niece anymore. So stay out of my life and I will stay out of yours."

CHAPTER TWENTY-FIVE
PAIGE AND PUSH

"You know after everything we've been through, I can't believe we actually did this shit," Push said looking into his wife's eyes, as she lay on top of him on the sand. They were both naked.

And although they were having fun and were no longer arguing, in the back of his mind he still felt she was harboring ill will. But Push tried to make the best of things, since they were in Mexico away from all the pussy he couldn't turn down no matter how hard he tried. He was really going to give the husband thing a try.

"Why you can't believe it?" she questioned kissing him softly on the lips as her breasts pressed against his bare chest.

"Because you may not believe this but I always wanted a family. And I always wanted you."

She laughed.

By Sante' Porter

"What's funny, babe?"

"Nothing," she smiled kissing him again, the breeze from the island caressing their bodies.

"Then why you laughing?"

"Because you've put me through so much," she said looking at him with hate. "More than a girl ever should have to go through."

He frowned and she rolled off his body. "I thought we worked things out."

"You the one who needed to work things out not me. I asked you, before we got together, the day you came to pick me up from the strip if you were ready and you said you were. But what did you do instead? Fuck this bitch and that bitch!"

"What you talking about, Paige?" he smiled a little worried at her tone.

"I'm talking about the phone stuffed in your pillow. I'm talking about the chick who texted you. And I'm talking about you being a liar! If it wasn't for you, I would've never been fucked up in the head!"

You Kissed Me, Now I Own You   187

He sat up and readjusted the towel under his body.

"What are you saying, Paige?"

"I'm saying you lied and I'm tired of liars."

Terror consumed him.

"So all of this was a lie? You married a nigga and brought me out here to fuck with my head?"

"No, to get your possessions and have them all in my name. Like they should be."

"So you're telling me you don't want to be with me?"

"Of course I wanted to be with you," she grinned. "But you couldn't be faithful. You had me in jail and because of it I lost my children for good. Now I want a life a way from you. A life with a better man and I'm going to get it too."

"So what now? Since you had me marry you on the strength of some bullshit!"

"Your trip in life ends here and I just wanted your view to be beautiful."

Push was confused, what had he done? And before he could think about it Paige removed a gun from her beach bag that she picked up as soon as they landed in Mexico. She

By Sante' Porter

didn't say a word more because her point was made. Instead she raised the barrel and killed him instantly.

Silencing him and his lying mouth forever, she watched him until his breath exited his body, blowing the sand. She wanted to be the last person on earth he saw. And when she was sure he was dead she walked naked to her bungalow off the water.

Without a care in the world she got dressed and caught a cab to the airport. It was time to move on with her life and she was going to do just that. The entire flight home she thought about how everything Push owned now belonged to her.

When she landed she was about to catch another cab when Exodus, a mid level drug dealer started following her in a black Mercedes truck. She thought it may have been one of Push's friends and decided she was done with running.

"What do you want?" She said loudly.

He smiled and rolled his window down. "Why the anger? You too beautiful for all of that."

"Who are you and why are you following me?"

Exodus didn't know whether to be frightened or turned on by Paige. She spoke to him with extreme authority and that was rare. "How did you know I was following you? I kept my distance."

"I saw you the moment I walked out the airport. Now what do you want?" She paused. "Why are you following me?"

"First off, the name's Exodus and I'm following you because you gonna be my wife," he said seriously. "Somebody as fine as you has to be on my arm."

Oh how she wished niggas stopped using that line.

"What makes you think that I'm not already somebody's wife? And furthermore, what makes you think I'd want anything to do with you?" Paige asked, no longer as angry. Besides, she wasn't as scared of him as she was when he first pulled up. Exodus was dangerously handsome; with his large brown eyes and sexy thug looks, and for some reason she wanted him like yesterday.

"I know you want me because you still standing here. And, I can look in your eyes, and tell that you're a hustler's

By Sante' Porter

wife. And since I'm in the business of making money I figured we can do the life thing together." He popped the lock. "Now let me take you to wherever you going."

With nothing else to do Paige looked around and eased inside of his truck. Before pulling off she said, "I'm gonna ask you three questions."

"Shoot." He leaned back and clasped his hands in front of him and examined the beauty.

"Are you feeling me?"

"So far."

She laughed. "Are you single? Because I don't have time for games."

He too thought it best to lie. "Mami, I haven't had a woman in two years so you can't get more single than that."

She thought it was weird but whatever. "Do you want a serious relationship? Somebody who will be in your corner and who would never leave you because she doesn't want to be alone."

Exodus wasn't for the tie down but he had to admit, mami was kind of cute. Before he could respond she raised her hand. "Don't lie to me, Exodus. Whatever you do, don't lie."

He was grown and although he could tell her to beat it, he decided to play along. He had time on his hands. "If you do right by me than you'll be the one. That's all I can say really."

She smiled. He would do just fine, as long as he acted right. "Then let's make it official. Kiss me."

"Official?" He chuckled. "Damn, you coming on strong."

"It's just a kiss. What can that hurt?"

The way he looked at it she was right. They were both grown so he kissed her. His mind told him she was off but her body was looking so tight.

It was a long kiss, one full of passion and he found himself wanting to have her immediately. After the kiss was over she said, "That was good, now you're mine."

By Sante' Porter

The Cartel Publications Order Form
www.thecartelpublications.com
Inmates **ONLY** receive novels for $10.00 per book.
(Mail Order **MUST** come from inmate directly to receive discount)

Shyt List 1	_____	$15.00
Shyt List 2	_____	$15.00
Shyt List 3	_____	$15.00
Shyt List 4	_____	$15.00
Shyt List 5	_____	$15.00
Pitbulls In A Skirt	_____	$15.00
Pitbulls In A Skirt 2	_____	$15.00
Pitbulls In A Skirt 3	_____	$15.00
Pitbulls In A Skirt 4	_____	$15.00
Victoria's Secret	_____	$15.00
Poison 1	_____	$15.00
Poison 2	_____	$15.00
Hell Razor Honeys	_____	$15.00
Hell Razor Honeys 2	_____	$15.00
A Hustler's Son 2	_____	$15.00
Black and Ugly	_____	$15.00
Black and Ugly As Ever	_____	$15.00
Year Of The Crackmom	_____	$15.00
Deadheads	_____	$15.00
The Face That Launched A	_____	$15.00
Thousand Bullets		
The Unusual Suspects	_____	$15.00
Miss Wayne & The Queens of DC	_____	$15.00
Paid In Blood (eBook Only)	_____	$15.00
Raunchy	_____	$15.00
Raunchy 2	_____	$15.00
Raunchy 3	_____	$15.00
Mad Maxxx	_____	$15.00
Quita's Dayscare Center	_____	$15.00
Quita's Dayscare Center 2	_____	$15.00
Pretty Kings	_____	$15.00
Pretty Kings 2	_____	$15.00
Pretty Kings 3	_____	$15.00
Silence Of The Nine	_____	$15.00
Silence Of The Nine 2	_____	$15.00
Prison Throne	_____	$15.00
Drunk & Hot Girls	_____	$15.00
Hersband Material	_____	$15.00
The End: How To Write A	_____	$15.00
Bestselling Novel In 30 Days (Non-Fiction Guide)		

You Kissed Me, Now I Own You   193

Upscale Kittens	_____	$15.00
Wake & Bake Boys	_____	$15.00
Young & Dumb	_____	$15.00
Young & Dumb 2:	_____	$15.00
Tranny 911	_____	$15.00
Tranny 911: Dixie's Rise	_____	$15.00
First Comes Love, Then Comes Murder	_____	$15.00
Luxury Tax	_____	$15.00
The Lying King	_____	$15.00
Crazy Kind Of Love	_____	$15.00
And They Call Me God	_____	$15.00
The Ungrateful Bastards	_____	$15.00
Lipstick Dom	_____	$15.00
A School of Dolls	_____	$15.00
KALI: Raunchy Relived	_____	$15.00
Skeezers	_____	$15.00
You Kissed Me, Now I Own You	_____	$15.00

Please add $4.00 **PER BOOK** for shipping and handling.

The Cartel Publications * P.O. BOX 486 OWINGS MILLS MD 21117

Name: _____

Address: _____

City/State: _____

Contact/Email: _____

Please allow 5-7 BUSINESS days before shipping.

The Cartel Publications is NOT responsible for prison orders rejected.

NO PERSONAL CHECKS ACCEPTED

STAMPS NO LONGER ACCEPTED

By Sante' Porter

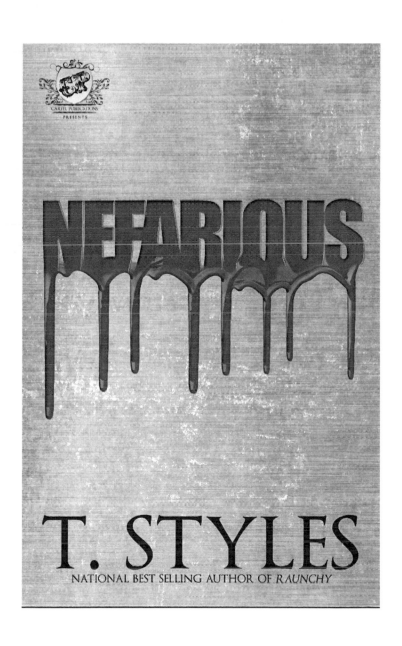